The Brotherhood
of the Yellow Beetle

G. H. Teed

Originally from *The Union Jack,*
Series 2, No. 507, June 28, 1913.

Stillwoods Edition, 2019.

Stillwoods.Blogspot.Ca

Catalogue Information:
Title: The Brotherhood of the Yellow Beetle
Author: G. H. Teed (1886-1938)
First published in: The Union Jack, Series 2, No. 507, June 28, 1913.
This Edition by: Stillwoods, 2019.
ISBN Canada: 978-1-988304-87-8
Blog: Stillwoods.Blogspot.Ca
Author Blog: http://ghteed.blogspot.com/
Storefront: http://www.lulu.com/spotlight/lulubook22

Keywords: Sexton Blake, British fictional detective, Wu Ling

Sir George Halliday, in China, is hunted by Wu Ling and The Brotherhood of the Yellow Beetle—to be killed before he can escape and return to England to warn the country about this criminal organization.

He does escape, but is killed back in England upon his arrival. Since he is a friend and confident of Sexton Blake, there is reason enough for the detective to pursue.

The inscrutable Orientals first kidnap Tinker and then Sir George's daughter. Their torture brings Blake to maddened heights of risk.

Bottom of Suez
Crooks' Vendetta
Voodoo Island
Five in Fear
The Grey Ghost
The Case of the Duplicate Key
The Temple of Many Visions
Gangland's Decree
The Clue of the Four Wigs
The Mystery of the Film City
The Black Abbot
Murder Ship
Spies Ltd.
A Mystery of the Big Woods
The Mystery of the Kidnapped Killer
The Secret of the Swamp
The Case of the Pink Macaw
The Terror of Gold-digger Creek
The Case of the Mummified Hand
Pearls of Doom
The Victim of the Gang
The Case of the Courtlandt Jewels
Nelson Lee and the Lhassa Red Menace
The Riddle of the Russian Gold
Voodoo Vengeance
Hounded Down
Bribery and Corruption
The Sacred Sphere
The Tiger of Canton
The Crook of Marsden Manor
The Affair of the Six Ikons
The Secret of the Coconut Groves
The Case of the Disguised Apache
Under the Eagle's Wing
The Rogues' Republic
The Mitcham Murder Mystery

CHAPTER I.   What Came Out of the Mist — The Vengeance of the Yellow Beetle — Sir George Halliday is Marked Down

The heavy evening mist was closing down with an almost sinister stealth over the yellow waters of Pe-chili Strait. Through the passage which is guarded on the one side by Port Arthur, and on the other by Wai-hai-wei, it came creeping from the Corea Bay and the Yellow Sea.

Instinct with all the mystery, the stealth, the cunning, and the deep inscrutable purpose of the teeming and changeless East it came, throwing, as it were, a protective blanket over the purposes and intentions of its children.

Into its capacious maw empty many rivers and streams — rivers which, like the long and winding Hwang-ho, pass through many different peoples and dissipate in their sweeping torrents the whisperings of night-born plots and deep Oriental passions.

Tiny and insignificant, in comparison, are the coast streams which hurry onward to the sea, but no less eloquent are they of mystery and stealth.

Why it is that the Celestial is so fond of the rivers and harbours for the conception of his plans and the pursuit of his purposes is a mystery; but so it is, from the water worshippers of the Ganges to the almost extinct swarthy pirates of the Malay Archipelago.

On the night in question, when the creeping mist had done its work, and only the lapping of the yellow water broke the stillness, there might have been seen stealing phantom-like through the night the form of a Chinese junk.

The guiding hand on the tiller evidently knew his way through the invisible waters as well as when they were lit by the orb of day, for straight and unhesitatingly she went, her sail barely bellied out by the dying breeze.

She had come from the direction of the Hwang-ho, and was heading south; not even when the wash of water on the shore became audible did she change her course. Rather, the helmsman guided her dead on the shore as the sound grew louder and louder, until suddenly it faded away into a distant murmur, and even through the mist could be seen the dark bulk of a river's bank, and below could be made out the placid waters of a river, indicating that, like the men who existed about it, they ran deep.

A hundred yards or more after he had left the waters of the gulf, and entered the river, the helmsman headed the junk for the bank. As though he had known the exact moment when the last puff of the fitful breeze would die out, he put the nose of the boat gently into the bank, just as the sail flapped slackly, and then hung still.

Until now, the man at the helm had been the only occupant of the deck of the junk; but, as though the slight jar of the boat against the bank had been a signal, another Chinaman suddenly appeared and leaped nimbly over the rail to the bank, a mooring-line in his hand.

Once the bow had been made fast, he turned his attention to the stern, and when that had also been secured, he squatted on his heels and silently rolled a cigarette.

The man at the helm hung as silently over the stern, watching, with impassive features, the waters beneath.

For half an hour the two sat thus before movement of any kind occurred. Then a shadowy figure loomed up out of the mist, and after exchanging a few muttered words with the man on the bank, stepped aboard and descended to the cabin below.

Hard on his heels another figure appeared. Again the low-toned colloquy took place, and he, like the other, silently stepped aboard and went below.

Another and another appeared, all stopping for a few words, and then disappearing after the others. Ten had come, and still the silent guard on the bank smoked on; still the man in the stern moved not.

Suddenly, however, the guard stirred slightly, and, throwing away his cigarette, got to his feet.

Simultaneously with his action came another figure through the mist — tall, cloaked, and with bent head. The guard bent himself with respectful submission, and as the last comer raised his head to speak in low tones, even through the mist one could feel, though not see, the power of his deep-set, inscrutable almond eyes.

He passed on and went below where the other ten were already seated. They stood up respectfully as he entered, and waited until he passed up to the other end, and squatted on the floor.

Then they followed his example, and waited for him to speak.

The so-called cabin was not a cabin in the strict sense of the word. What its original disposition had been, it would be hard to say; but now it was a long, low compartment, without table and without chairs.

The floor itself was covered with a thick grass carpet on which were carelessly thrown thick, vivid-toned rugs. Along the floor, close to the walls, were heaps of silken cushions, rivalling in their gorgeous tints the rugs beyond.

Overhead, the rough beams of the deck of the junk contrasted in dark-toned bulk with the colour below, while, if there ever had been windows, they were obscured by the heavy silken hangings of rich, blazing yellow, which covered every inch of the walls.

Seated down each side on the cushions were the ten men who had first arrived.

Alone, at the other end, and squatting on a yellow cushion, was the man who had entered last. A big, swinging lamp lit up the scene below, and by its light could be seen the power of the eyes which above could only be felt.

His head was close-cropped like that of the European, and by its shape and poise, the head was that of the thinker and student, while the thin, yellow hands and square, slightly bulging lines of the jaw indicated the practical and determined.

The brow was high and broad, and though in repose, the face might have been earnest, cruel, or what not, for all one could read in its expression. He had neither beard nor moustache, and on his hands wore no jewellery of any description, with the exception of a blazing yellow topaz on the little finger of his left. His clothes were rich, and a blend of blue and yellow, while gleaming against his tunic was a glittering, jewelled order.

Before him was set a low, desk-like affair, containing modern pens, with a supply of thin parchment-paper, and a pot of ink. Before speaking, he bent over and inspected them, and then, lifting his head, he glanced slowly and piercingly at each man who sat there.

They were, by their dress, of all stations in life — some wearing the rich costume of the wealthy mandarin, while one, at the far end, wore a coarse suit of blue cotton.

It seemed not to affect the man at the other end, however, for as his eyes passed over the cheap garments, his expression altered not a whit. For the tiniest fraction of a second, his glance lingered on a stout, richly-dressed mandarin sitting near him, then it passed on, finally to come to rest again on the low desk in front of him.

Suddenly he raised his head, and, looking at the stout mandarin, spoke, his tone coming in soft, liquid accents, pregnant with force.

3

"A week ago, we, the Brethren of the Yellow Beetle, met here. Then we deputed you, Foo Loo, to carry out the decision of the council which was a step in our great campaign. Tonight you were to bring us news of your success. Speak!"

The stout mandarin listened, as though fascinated, to the slow words of the other. His brow showed first a tiny bead of sweat, then another and another, until there were a host of them. He struggled to speak, but seemed held by the fascination of the other's gaze.

"Does Wu Ling, the head of the Yellow Beetle, need to order twice?" asked the man at the upper end, as the mandarin failed to open his lips.

As though the menacing quiet of the words had unlocked his jaws, Foo Loo, the mandarin, rose and walked up between his seated companions until he stood before the desk. Then, dropping to his knees, he bowed his head and spoke.

"Oh, illustrious one, head of the most favoured and exalted Yellow Beetle, your unworthy and not-to-be-mentioned creature craves your indulgence."

"Away with such preamble!" replied Wu Ling impassively. 'Speak!'

"Oh, Excellency, I went as the council ordered. I spent money as water in an effort to carry out the purposes of the council against the English pig. I failed, however, for he got away and is even now on his way to England!"

For a moment Wu Ling's eyes closed as though to conceal the hidden fire which blazed forth at the news he had heard. Then he slowly opened them, and his voice was toneless as ever as he spoke.

"So, Foo Loo, you have failed to carry out the orders of the council?"

"Yes, Excellency, and I beg for the leniency of the council. If given more time I can achieve the purpose."

Wu Ling seemed not to have heard him, for he gazed over his head at the others.

"Brethren of the Yellow Beetle," he said slowly, "there are three men — English pigs, if you will — who know the great purpose of the council. Two left China and made their way to England before we knew of their knowledge. The third, however, Sir George Halliday, was still here. By the method of the council we drew lots to see who should put him out of the way. It was too important a matter to trust to a mere agent. It was imperative that it should be done. Foo Loo drew the straw which appointed him to do our will. He has failed. He comes to us and begs for leniency, while the man who possesses our secret is on his way to England."

"But, Excellency," broke in Foo Loo, "I looked for him as a passenger, nor did I know until late that he had escaped by disguising as a stoker."

"The council is not dealing in excuses, Foo Loo,' replied Wu Ling impassively. Then, looking at the others, he continued: 'Brethren, what is your verdict?"

A low rumble sounded as the answer came: 'The Beetle.'

Wu Ling turned back to the kneeling mandarin.

"You hear?" he asked softly.

The mandarin bowed his head in silence. Then Wu Ling thrust his hand into the folds of his rich tunic, and when he drew it out it held a tiny metal case.

Silently he held it out. Foo Loo, with fascinated gaze and trembling hand, reached out and took it.

For a moment he gazed at it fearfully and turned appealingly to the assembled council. Only impassive countenances met him on every side, however, and with trembling knees he rose.

Slowly he made his way down the centre of the cabin until he reached the farther end where the heavy silken curtain hid the entrance to the companion-way. Then he turned and once more dropped to his knees.

His yellow face worked convulsively as his trembling fingers forced the cover off the metal case. Inside was a piece of cotton wool, from which came the odour of a heavy, pungent perfume. Setting the box on the carpet in front of him Foo Loo bared his throat and, lifting the saturated bit of cotton-wool, wiped it over the throat from chin to chest. Then he replaced it in the box and closed the cover. Once more he looked appealingly at Wu Ling, who made no sign.

With a choking gurgle Foo Loo again lifted the box and in the bottom pressed an invisible spring.

The first sign of expression passed over the faces of the watchers as the bottom flew open and there dropped on the carpet a small shining beetle of pure, brilliant yellow. Its vivid tones were those of the silken curtains and cushions, the yellow of Wu Ling's tunic and the deep tone of the topaz which blazed on his hand.

For a moment the tiny beetle seemed dazed by its sudden entry into the lighted room, but as the pungent odour of the perfume smeared on Foo Loo's throat caught its senses, it slowly turned and lifted its pin-like head from which projected a needle-like point fully a quarter of an inch in length.

The mandarin gazed in speechless horror, and shuddered as the beetle waved the needle-like point slowly about; then, as it began moving forward with a soft, metallic rustle of its scales, he closed his eyes and waited with clutched hands.

Foo Loo opened his eyes, saw it coming, and gave a stifled shriek as he dropped forward on his face and lay still.

For a few moments the watchers sat there, waiting for a sign from Wu Ling. Finally he raised his hand, and pointed at the coolie who sat near the fallen, crumpled figure of Foo Loo.

There was no need for him to speak. The man knew only too well what was required of him. Rising quickly, he moved noiselessly across to the body, and with a deft movement threw Foo Loo back on his shoulders.

It was hard to believe that the still face had been working so convulsively a moment before, and that one touch of the needle-like point of the Yellow Beetle had killed him so suddenly. Against his throat was a dark point, sole proof that he had died other than a normal death.

As for the beetle, it had dropped to the carpet and was running about blindly, drunkenly, drugged into harmlessness by the pungent perfume, but not until it had achieved its intended purpose.

Drawing the metal box to him the coolie pressed the spring in the bottom. Then, picking up the dazed beetle, he dropped it in the opening, its scales rattling harshly as it flapped feebly against the steel sides.

With a click he closed the box and walked up to Wu Ling, who took it in silence and returned it to his tunic.

The coolie moved noiselessly back to the hangings over the companion-way. There he drew them aside and sent a guttural hail up to the deck.

A moment later the man who had been there on guard and the helmsman appeared.

The coolie spoke not, but pointed to the body.

Silently they bent and lifted it up, and when they had gained the deck a soft splash in the mist-laden waters was the last act in the evening's brief drama.

When the deck-hands had disappeared with Foo Loo, the coolie dropped the hangings, and, after bowing to Wu Ling, squatted once more in his place by the wall.

All eyes sought the features of Wu Ling, and it is safe to say that, inscrutable as were their features outwardly, inwardly they were consumed with curiosity as to what he had to say.

Not without a full knowledge of the rules of the Brotherhood of the Yellow Beetle had those men of every class gained the Inner Council. Not without being prepared unhesitatingly to fulfil their self-inflicted doom should they fail to carry out any of the decrees of the man who wielded a power many kings might envy.

One and all, they would stop at nothing to obey orders, and in the pursuance of such even should father, brother, or friend be an obstruction, they would swiftly be removed.

After a silence of some moments Wu Ling opened his eyes and began speaking in his low tones, which, for all their liquid softness, reached every man there.

"Brethren," he said, "you have seen the reward of failure. Foo Loo was my friend, and now that he is gone I send him my blessing. But, were he my brother, were he my father, were he myself, the penalty for failure must be paid. In our great purpose no man, no thing, must stop us. We have set ourselves a purpose, and with the aid of the blessed and all-wise Confucius, will we be victorious.

"Our illustrious race, which has rested for centuries in the reflected glory of Confucius, shall now by the guiding of Wu Ling, most unworthy though I be, go on until the white races, who have in their vanity spurned us and oppressed us, are under the heel of the East.

"I, Wu Ling, say it shall be so. I have spent years in their cities and houses of learning, preparing for the great day, and now the day is at hand. First must we find and crush by the Yellow Beetle the three men who have escaped to England with a knowledge of our secrets and purposes.

"The man who betrayed us has met with a just punishment, as has Foo Loo tonight, but those men must be removed. I myself —I, Wu Ling, the head of the illustrious Brotherhood of the Yellow Beetle, will lead the campaign in person. And you, my brethren, will follow me. That is all. If you would ask anything of me, speak!"

A dead silence rested for some moment over the assembled men, but finally a man in rich garb rose, and bowed low.

"Most illustrious one," he said, "your unworthy servant would ask a question."

"Speak!" said Wu Ling.

"Is it of thy purpose, O illustrious one, to tell us more of your plans?"

Wu Ling waved his hand.

"Be seated, I will tell you. I go to London, and you, my brethren, come also. There, we first remove the men who bear our secret, and if others have gained possession of it we will remove them also. Then, my brethren, will we create a reign of terror throughout the land of the white pigs until they meet our demands. And may Confucius bless our efforts by the blessing of the Three Lakes and the Four Moons."

All heads bowed again as Wu Ling finished, and then he rose. Celestial though he was, he was the highest expression of dignity and majesty as he passed down between the bowed heads and drew aside the yellow silken hangings over the entrance to the companion-way. There he turned, and spoke in soft, guttural accents.

"Brethren, remember the Yellow Beetle!"

A moment later he was gone, and with his departure the remaining nine lifted their heads and rose. One by one they passed out silently behind him, until last of all the man in coolie garb dropped the curtain and disappeared.

In blazing yellow silence was the cabin left, the stillness only broken a few minutes later by the gentle waving to and fro of the wall-hangings, as the crew of two got out long sweeps and propelled the little junk along with the current to try and catch some of the night breeze in the open sea beyond.

In silence — yes, for half-an-hour the cabin showed no signs of movement except the curtains. Suddenly, however, up at the far end, directly behind where Wu Ling had sat, the yellow hanging was pushed aside stealthily, one eye appeared, and then a tousled black head.

Slowly, and peering about cautiously the while, the head came further and further into view until it was entirely clear of the curtains — the head, the eyes, the skin of a white man — an Englishman.

His hair was tangled, his face smutted with soot and grease, and his clothes consisted only of greasy black overalls and jumper, but the prominent nose, clean-cut chin, and independent poise of the head betokened the ruler and law-maker.

Clever as the now departed Foo Loo had thought himself, and in spite of the money he had spent in order to remove Sir George Halliday before he got out of China, his efforts had been fruitless, and he had paid the penalty.

But when he said Sir George had disguised himself as a stoker he was only partly right. True, Sir George had disguised himself as a stoker, but had only remained on board the steamer during her stay in port. Foo Loo's men, hot on his trail, had driven him at the last moment to throw up his intention.

In a situation where he could not seek assistance, and with half a dozen bloodthirsty Chinamen at his heels, he had taken to the docks. From there the chase had led across the decks of a tangled mass of junks until the pursuers had been baffled by the sudden disappearance of their quarry.

As the spot where he had disappeared was near the liner, and as at that moment the big steamer had slipped her mooring, they concluded he had in some way regained her deck, and was on his way to England.

Not so, however, for Sir George had tumbled down the first open companion-way he saw. On his arrival at the bottom he had turned, expecting every moment would bring the yellow fiends down after him, but as minute succeeded minute, and still they did not come, he began to breathe more freely. Had he, after all, shaken them off, or had they with true diabolical cunning set themselves to wait there, knowing he could not escape?

He had been surprised to find a soft curtain hung before the entrance to the cabin. From the feel of it he knew it was silk, and it was not usual for coastal junks to go about with silken-hung cabins. Passing his hands along the walls in his search for a window or porthole of some description through which he might find an avenue of escape, he marvelled still more at the continuation clear around of the silk.

Once he stumbled, and, finding the object which he had struck, whistled softly at feeling a pile of soft, luxurious cushions.

"Gad!" he muttered. "It seems as though I'd struck some sort of a portable harem. I'll be worse off than ever if I'm caught nosing about in here, for it certainly is not an ordinary junk. I wonder what the deuce it is used for."

At that moment the noise of a soft slushing step on the staircase caught his ear, and grabbing at the silken hangings he slipped behind, and stood close against the wall.

Lucky was it for him that a heavy supporting stanchion passed down there, and by standing stiff and straight he did not bulge the curtain at all.

A moment later a dim yellow gleam came through the hangings, but what the new arrival was doing he could not guess. Then he had put out the light, and departed, leaving Sir George once more alone.

He dared not move, however, for fear of discovery, and cramped as was the position, he was compelled to keep it all through the night.

Dawn found him stiff, sore, and haggard, but disregarding his physical discomfort, he drew aside the hangings and peered out.

The cabin was still shadowy and dim, but the curtain over the entrance to the companion-way had been thrust aside, and some daylight filtered in. He was too astonished for words as he found himself gazing out on the luxurious cabin where Wu Ling met the council of the Yellow Beetle, and which was that coming night to witness the self-inflicted death of Foo Loo.

Steps on the deck overhead warned Sir George that people were about, and soon the moving of the junk told him it was under way. Such a physical strain had he gone through the past few days during his strenuous attempts to escape from the vendetta which had been proclaimed against him that, dangerous as was his position now, it was impossible for him to remain awake any longer.

He surreptitiously pushed aside the hangings, drew a pile of cushions in nearer, in order to hide the bulge, and then, casting himself down as close to the wall as he could, in less than a minute he was sound asleep. What providence watched over him during that long day it is hard to say, but when he awoke it was evening.

The junk still held on her way, as he knew from the gentle rolling; but whither they were bound he had no idea. He was ravenously hungry, but ruefully decided that for the moment the question of food must be put aside. The junk might come to an anchor during the evening, and then he might find some means of escape.

Cautiously he pushed the curtains back where they had been, and once more took up his position close to the wall. Then his hopes had been raised by feeling the motion of the junk almost cease, and he had lost no time in making his preparations.

Just as he was about to push aside the hangings and investigate matters a shuffling footstep sounded, and once more the cabin was flooded with light. Then the footsteps departed, the junk stopped entirely, and Sir George knew from the faint noise overhead that she was being moored.

Once more he was about to make a bid for freedom, when another interruption occurred. It was the first of the council to arrive, and the man in hiding puzzled his mind in futile conjecture as Chinaman after Chinaman arrived. It was the gathering of the council whose doings that night have already been related.

Sir George Halliday was a man who knew China better than most white men, and who spoke the language like a native. Like the intrepid Sven Hedin he had traversed Tibet and the Himalayas, looking for the elusive source of the Brahmaputra. He had followed the brave and gallant Bruce on that long, tortuous journey from Leh overland to Peking, crossing on his way to the extreme north-west corner of Tibet.

Qualities which made such hazardous trips possible had been, however, coalesced into a single aim by the incentive of his desire to become an authority on the hidden, mysterious country and peoples through which he passed.

There he had heard faint whisperings of a force — a mighty, all-powerful force — which eventually was to sweep Christendom from the face of the globe. Once, and once only, had he heard used the expression, 'Yellow Beetle', but more than that all his diplomacy, all his knowledge of the language, and all his offers of gold failed to tell him.

In Peking, however, he had gained more knowledge of the secrets of the mysterious organisation, but before he could follow it up his informant had met the vengeance of the Yellow Beetle. Then had started the persistent attempts to put him out of the way before he could reach the comparative safety of England.

These efforts he had so far, however, eluded, until the wheel of Fate had so strangely cast him behind the silken curtains of the very cabin in which a meeting of the Brotherhood was being held — a night on which Wu Ling himself, the very source of the organisation which had spread its tentacles around the world, had outlined to the council his plans for the future.

He had seen too many horrors in China to be much affected by Foo Loo's death, but the sinister rustle of the beetle's scales had sent a cold shiver up his spine. Had any of that inscrutable council known of his presence in the very heart of the organisation, his death would have been slow and lingering, but none the less certain.

However, by an almost superhuman effort to stand motionless, we have seen how he succeeded. Now, after peering cautiously about, he stepped forth, and stood beside where the powerful Wu Ling had just been sitting. If he could only get out of his present position he was in possession of information which no other white man had.

The two others spoken of by Wu Ling would possess no more than he had had, if as much. But now he knew the colossal and gigantic plan of the organisation which had been so carefully built up, and it behoved him to get to England as quickly as possible. His thoughts were interrupted by the sound of a shuffling footstep, but this time, instead of slipping back behind the curtain, he sped quickly down to the other end, and concealed himself there just as the curtain over the door was thrust aside, and the deck hand entered. He walked straight up to the hanging lamp, and, lowering it by a cord, turned it out. Then he drew it up again, and turned to find his way out.

As his shuffling steps drew nearer and nearer, the man in hiding quickly formed a plan. It would require swift, sure action, but that must be risked. He was determined to escape at all costs, and could hardly risk more than he had already done, he thought grimly.

Nearer and nearer drew the steps until the silken hangings behind which he stood fluttered slightly from contact with the passing Chinaman's sleeve.

Then Sir George acted, and acted quickly. Without pausing to thrust aside the hangings, he leaped forward, a ripping, tearing sound following as the hangings gave. Heedless of this he hurled himself blindly at the startled Chinaman, who had gasped sharply at the noise.

Rather than a hindrance the curtain was of use to Sir George, for it fell over the head of the Celestial, hindering his movements materially. As Sir George's hands felt the other's throat, he closed them convulsively, and then began a silent, deadly struggle in the darkness, neither man being able to see his opponent.

Up the full length of the cabin the fight raged, and then back again. Weak though he was for want of food, Sir George was fighting with the strength of desperation.

As for the Celestial, he knew every trick which was used from Batavia to Shanghai, and he made use of them. The Englishman, however, relaxed his grip not an atom, and as for the second time they reached the upper end of the cabin the Chinaman yielded to the pressure.

There was an ominous crack in his arm as Sir George hurled him to the floor, but the victor spent no time in finding out the cause. Quickly he stripped the clothes from the unconscious Celestial, and after taking off his own greasy overalls, put the others on.

The overalls he put on the Celestial, and then, with strips of the yellow curtain, bound him. The same material served as a ball for a gag, and after sticking the Chinaman's kris in his waistband, he moved cautiously towards the companion-way, and ascended to the deck.

The mist was gone, the stars hung low and large in a purple sky; the moon beat down in cold unconcern, her disc as yellow as the curtains back in the cabin. Leaning indolently over the tiller was the helmsman, and forward the sail flapped in the growing breeze.

On each side Sir George could see the banks of a river, but even as he looked the current swept them out into the open gulf, the sail bellied out, and the helmsman put her head for the north.

All this he saw in a moment, and then, adopting the shuffling step of the Celestial, he made his way towards the stern. The helmsman took no notice of his approach until Sir George was close upon him. It was then he saw the difference between his fellow and the newcomer.

Without hesitating the fraction of a second, or inquiring as to the why and the wherefore, he dropped the tiller, drew his crooked-bladed knife, and sprang forward.

Sir George expected a struggle, but had hardly looked for such a sudden onslaught as this. He thanked his stars in that moment that he had brought the other's knife with him. Springing back, he drew it, and jabbed it up to the guard, while the junk, free of control, brought up dangerously before the wind and headed for the shore.

The helmsman was shrewd enough to know that a stranger dressed in the garb of his shipmate and in possession of his knife was of a dangerous calibre, and as the pale light of the moon flashed from the knife-blade to Sir George's face the Celestial's eyes narrowed as he saw his antagonist was a white man.

Hurling himself forward, he slashed viciously at the other's guard, a dripping flow of vivid red showing where the point of his blade got home.

The Englishman, however, had been waiting for just such a move, and barely had the other's knife ripped his arm than he had an iron hold on the wrist. Then, struggling and straining, he threw his injured arm up and down with lightning rapidity in an endeavour to escape the attempted clutch of the Chinaman.

Back and forth across the deck they went until a vicious roll of the junk hurled them both half senseless against the side. Driven on by the shock, the helmsman's guard drove back, weighted by Sir George's grip; the crooked blade turned sharply, and as they crashed together, by his own hand was the Chinaman's knife driven to his heart.

Another violent roll sent them reeling backwards, and as Sir George pushed free, the return of the junk threw the Celestial against the low rail, and with a slanting somersault he tumbled over the rail.

Shaken by the accidental result of the fight, Sir George dropped his own blade and leaped for the tiller. As he sent the junk's head round and the sail slowly filled he held his breath.

The shore was barely ten yards away, and he expected every moment to feel her go bumping on the rocks. Indeed, as she came round, he felt an ominous quiver run along her hull as she grazed a hidden boulder; but the sail filled out, and, carried by the breeze, she swung clear.

How he ever made his way out of the gulf past Wei-hai-wei and down through the Yellow Sea to Shanghai Sir George never knew. He was crew, captain, and cook all in one, and small as the junk was, it was no sinecure.

Had the weather been rough he would never have made it, but several days later he floated in through a tangled conglomeration of steamers, junks, and sampans, and after recklessly tying up the junk, made his way, more dead than alive, to a big liner about to sail for England, realising full well the strength of the sinister power which was on his heels.

"Going out, guv'nor?"

Tinker asked the question and looked up as his master emerged from his dressing-room clad in evening-clothes.

"Yes, my lad," replied Blake thoughtfully. "I'm going round to Sir George Halliday's for dinner, and I am afraid my writing has kept me late. However, I'll get a taxi, and will not be long reaching there."

"Not a case is it, guv'nor?"

"I don't know yet," said Blake absently, as he selected a cigar and lit it. "Sir George wrote me a note asking me to drop round to dinner, and saying, incidentally, that he had something of interest to tell me. It may not be anything but some inside information regarding developments in the East. He has just arrived from China, you know."

"Oh, yes; I remember, guv'nor. Isn't he the man who has done so much exploration work out there?"

"Yes, indeed!" answered Blake warmly. "He has added much to our knowledge of Tibet and Turkestan, as well as Central China; and if, as I think, he has some fresh notes, I look forward keenly to reading them. However, I must be getting along. Hallo! I wonder who that is?"

This, as an agitated ringing came at the street door.

"Just see who it is, my lad," added Blake, with a frown of irritation. "I hope it isn't a professional call."

Tinker slipped out of his chair and left the consulting-room to answer the door. From where he stood Blake heard the hurried question of an excited voice, and then hasty steps came down the passage. A moment later the door opened, and there dashed in a tall, well-dressed young man in an evident state of great agitation.

"Mr. Blake?" he asked excitedly, almost chopping off Tinker's nose as he unthinkingly banged the door after him.

"Yes," replied Blake calmly. "But might I ask—"

"Yes, yes!" cried the newcomer, sinking into a chair. "I'll tell you everything as we go along! Can you come at once?"

"Look here!" remarked Blake. "Get a grip on yourself, man, and speak more definitely. You rush in here like a wild man, and ask me to go to some place with you, neither saying where nor on what business. You are taking my consent for granted, which is not yet given. Now, if you will favour me with your name and try and tell me the cause of your excitement, perhaps I can be of assistance to you. If not" — and Blake shrugged — "I am afraid I must ask you to excuse me, for I am on my way to fulfil a dinner engagement."

As though suddenly sobered by the cold douche of Blake's remarks, the other straightened up, and passed his hand across his brow.

"Yes, yes," he muttered; "you are right, Mr. Blake. I apologise, but for a moment the awful thing that has happened drove everything else from my mind."

"Well," interrupted Blake curtly, "please get to the point."

"It is this," responded the other. "First, I will tell you my name is Carslake — Godfrey Carslake. I — I am the affianced husband of Miss Halliday— Sir George Halliday's only daughter. Oh, it is too terrible!" he muttered, breaking off.

"Ah!" remarked Blake quickly. "Sir George Halliday, you say? Is the trouble connected with him?"

The other nodded.

"Yes — he — is — dead!"

"What!" snapped Blake, leaning forward tensely. "Sir George Halliday, the Asiatic explorer, dead?"

"Yes," responded Carslake; "dead. He died less than an hour ago, and the doctor whom we called pronounced it heart-failure. But — but both Miss Halliday and myself think that in some way there has been foul play."

"Wait!" interrupted Blake. "Tell me the details in the taxi. Tinker, get my hat and coat. Bring Pedro. Look alive!" Then, turning to Carslake, he said: "It is a very strange coincidence. I was just on my way to dine with him."

Carslake nodded.

"Yes, I know; the butler told me. I had forgotten before to mention that that was the reason of my coming to you at once. I thought Sir George might have intended consulting you about matters."

"About matters!" jerked Blake, remembering Sir George had said in his note he desired to tell him something. "What matters?"

Carslake shook his head.

"That's it," he replied. "I don't know what; but of this I am convinced. There has been foul play, although the doctor scouts any such idea."

At that moment Tinker returned with Blake's hat and coat, and five minutes later the whole party, with Pedro, were in a taxi heading at a smart pace for Sir George's house.

"Now then," said Blake, as the driver turned out of Baker Street. "I think you said you were engaged to Miss Halliday?"

"Yes; only since last evening, though. You see, while Sir George was in China his daughter stayed with her aunt, and although there was an understanding between us there was nothing definite. We were waiting for her father's return. As you know, he arrived last week, and in order to let him get over the fatigue of the journey I didn't speak to him until last night.

"He was very nice about it, and said he had no objection, but before permitting an announcement he said he felt in duty bound to tell me of a peril which was hanging over him, and which he was afraid might hang over his daughter unless he were able to change conditions soon. Of course I thought he might be exaggerating, and told him I didn't care what the peril was, and that as my wife, Gertrude his daughter, would be entitled to my protection.

"After leaving him, however, I saw Gertrude and told her what he had said. Instead of looking at it as I did, she grew very frightened and told me that ever since her father's return he had been very oppressed and worried. The upshot was that he arranged to tell me what it was tonight after dinner, and I can only think now he intended to tell you as well."

Blake nodded.

"Yes; I have no doubt of it. However, go on, please."

"There is not much more to tell," went on Carslake. "Sir George was in his study, writing before dinner, while Gertrude and I were in the drawing-room. We didn't know then that you were coming to dinner. It seems, however, that the butler went to the study to inquire of his master as to when he expected you to arrive.

"The next thing, he had come tearing into the drawing room, his face as white as chalk, and his eyes wide with horror. I saw at once there was something wrong, and hurried out to the study. The moment I entered I saw what it was."

Carslake again passed his hand over his brow, and then continued: "Sir George was sitting at his desk just as though he had fallen asleep. His right hand still grasped the pen, while his left was clenched tightly and lay curled up under his head, which rested on it as though in sleep. Two letters were sealed and addressed, while the sheet ot paper before him contained only the date written on it.

"I sent for a doctor at once, but it was plain to be seen he was dead. The doctor called it heart failure, and said the very fact that he was in the act of writing a letter precluded all possibility of the suicide theory. Besides, he said his lips gave off not the slightest odour of any drug or poison. Foul play he scouted at once, saying everything pointed to that as being impossible; but, in view of what he told me, both Gertrude and myself feel we would like you to make an examination."

"She is, of course, very much broken up?" remarked Blake.

"Completely prostrated," replied Carslake. "She and her father were very fond of one another."

"You say there were no signs of violence?" said Blake, after a short pause.

"Not the faintest. Certainly, everything points to a natural death, and now that I am calmer I am beginning to wonder myself if perhaps, after all, Gertrude and I have not built too quickly on our fears."

"That remains to be seen," answered Blake, as the taxi stopped. "However, here we are. I'll make an examination at once."

Carslake led the way up the steps and pressed the button of the electric-bell. The door was opened almost at once by the butler, whose face still bore traces of the shock through which he had passed. Miss Halliday was not to be seen, and the butler, in answer to Carslake's question, informed him in a whisper that, before leaving, the doctor had given her an opiate, and that now she was sleeping.

"This is Mr. Blake," went on Carslake. "He desires to make an examination."

"Yes, sir," replied the old servant, looking with respect at the brilliant criminologist. "Shall I go with you, sir, or do you prefer to go alone?"

"Has the room been disturbed?" asked Blake, speaking for the first time since entering the house.

"No, sir. Only Sir George" — and the old butler's voice broke — "has been moved, sir. The doctor ordered us to lay him on the couch."

"Very well," replied Blake. "If you will lead the way, Carslake, we will lose no time. You, Tinker, keep Pedro here in the hall for the present."

Tinker pulled Pedro back and sat down on a big oak seat, while Carslake led the way to Sir George's study.

It was more of an elaborate library than a study, its tones being a restful shade of deep crimson. Around the walls were bookcases packed with what Blake knew was one of the finest collections of books in London.

At one end was a huge open fireplace, and to the right of this stood a massive, flat-topped mahogany desk — the one at which the ill-fated baronet had been writing when he was so suddenly struck down. Against the wall, to the left of the door on entering, was a big leather couch, on which lay the man, calm and peaceful, who a bare hour before had been full of vigorous life.

For a moment Blake stood on the threshold of the room and cast his keen eyes rapidly about. Then they lingered on the deep alcove straight across, where long French windows opened on to a wide balcony which overlooked a series of terraces leading to a garden, and thence to the high stone wall which separated Sir George's grounds from the lane at the rear.

Then Blake turned his attention to the man whose guest he had started out to be. Reverently lifting the hands, he made a close examination of the palms and nails, but even with the aid of the powerful pocket-glass he had brought, they were perfectly normal in appearance. From the hands he transferred his attention to the head, running his long, sensitive fingers over the thinly-covered scalp. No bump, no abrasion could he find.

Then slowly, and with the utmost care, he again picked up the glass and began a most minute examination of the features. Over brow and eyes he worked slowly and patiently until he had covered every particle. Then he shifted the glass to the cheeks and lips. From ear to ear he turned his gaze, but as he passed the glass along the rim of the lower lip, he suddenly paused and leaned forward intently.

Magnified by the glass, he saw a tiny yellow spot, which was so small that it would be almost certain to escape the naked eye.

But it was not the tiny yellow spot only which caused him to lean forward, but what he saw in the very centre of it. There, rimmed by the yellow, was an infinitesimal black puncture, which for all the world looked as though the point of the finest of fine needles had touched the lip.

There was nothing remarkable in a man having a tiny puncture in his skin, but such a minute hole would, in the ordinary course of events, heal up very quickly in a normally healthy man, and Sir George Halliday had been more than that — he had been robust.

Even as he looked, Blake knew the puncture, from its appearance, must be less than half a dozen hours old; but whether such an innocent-looking mark had anything to do with Sir George's death he had no idea. It seemed highly improbable; but, true to his capacity for details, Blake stored the point in his mind and turned his attention to the throat.

For fully an hour he worked ceaselessly, examining the dead man minutely; but, when he finally straightened up, he had to confess to himself that, beyond the tiny, almost invisible mark on the lip, he had found nothing, and that the doctor's conclusions didn't seem hastily formed. He merely grunted in answer to Carslake's anxious questions, and waving him curtly aside, turned his attention to the desk.

It had very little on it. A heavy silver inkstand, several pens in a tray, a large blue pencil, and square blotting-pad, the top sheet of which had been only slightly used.

To the left of where the writer would sit were two letters, while lying on the blotting-pad, just as it had been when death so suddenly overtook the writer, was a sheet of heavy paper containing only the date — or, to be more correct, nearly all the date, for at the very last figure the writing trailed off in a shaky, blotted line where the pen had faltered.

Beside the sheet of paper was the pen with which Sir George had been writing, but beyond that neither desk nor chair showed anything else, and least of all anything of a suspicious nature. Blake sank into the chair and leaned his elbows on the desk.

For some time he sat in deep thought, his eyes closed, his chest barely rising and falling as he breathed lightly. Then he opened his eyes, picked up the pen, and took — as far as he could judge — the position which would have been assumed by Sir George. Placing the point of the pen at the last number of the date on the paper, he began a slow scrutiny of the room. First the desk before him, then the walls, the ceiling, and the floor on either side.

From that his eyes wandered to the huge fireplace, and thence to the deep embrasure of the window. Carslake followed each movement with puzzled and expectant eyes, but looked still more so when Blake laid down the pen and stood up.

"I presume Miss Halliday would not object to my reading the addresses of these two letters?" asked Blake in low tones.

"Oh, no, indeed!" replied Carslake: "She would be glad to have you do anything which will clear up matters. But tell me, Mr. Blake, do you consider Sir George's death was after all a natural one?"

Blake shrugged.

"My dear fellow, what impossible questions you do ask! The doctor scouts any such idea, while the only suggestion of foul play emanates from you and Miss Halliday, and is based on Sir George's harassed manner since his return, as well as by some mysterious peril which he told you was hanging over him, and which, by the way, he would have confided to you tonight had death not intervened. The point is, Carslake, was this peril real or supposed, of a physical, mental, or momentary nature? What was its cause — its cause — do you understand?

"Sir George no doubt had something of moment to tell, for, as well as confiding in you, his future son-in-law, he thought it wise to confide in me as well. Does that pre-suppose a peril of a physical nature and of such severity as to cause his death? At present there is just one point, Carslake, which could possibly be attributed to an outside source, but it is so infinitesimal that I hesitate to base much upon it.

"With your leave, however, I shall now proceed to make a minute examination of everything in the room, and beg of you to touch nothing, least of all anything on the desk. If any outside agent was the cause of Sir George's death, it must, by the very nature of things, have come into the vicinity of the desk, and perhaps has still left some trail — who knows? It is a pity we do not know the peril to which Sir George referred, for, knowing that, we would sooner or later be able to put our fingers on the motive — the motive, Carslake, which generated the cause and leaves its mark in the effect which we see before us in the form of my old friend.

"Now let us see to whom Sir George was writing. Ah! as I thought, he has come home with some fresh notes on China, for this one is addressed to "The Chinese and Tibetan Research Society", of which I believe he was a fellow, and at one time its president. The other, I see, is to the publishing firm of Dobbs, Milne & Co., who, as you know, specialise in scientific publications.

"If you will send for the butler, Carslake, we will have these letters posted at once, and in the morning I shall go around to both places and ask to be shown the contents. By one of those hidden elements of chance, that on which Sir George was occupied when death came may serve to throw some light on our investigations.

With this, Blake picked up his pocket-glass, and shifting the light to the required angle, dropped to his knees. Those who have followed Sexton Blake's methods will be familiar with his mode of procedure on this occasion. With his usual care for detail, he mapped out the zone for examination in a series of imaginary squares. In this way every detail of the carpeted floor was brought under the glass, and did the tiniest bit of the map show any discoloration or other sign out of the ordinary, the keen eyes of the detective would pick it out at once and dissect it.

Floor, chairs, tables, and walls gave no indication of any extraordinary condition, however, and Blake, with a muttered remark, turned and contemplated the big fireplace. On the dogs lay three immense logs which by force of their heat precluded, in Blake's mind, any chance of a hostile entry from that source.

There was nothing left now but the window, and signing to Carslake to throw the light around, Blake entered the deep recess and began to examine the catch. Barely had he focused the glass on it, however, when he leaned forward quickly and drew a sharp breath.

To the ordinary observer there was nothing in its appearance to cause comment. Its composition was of brass-finished metal, and consisted of two parts, the catch being on one sash and the bolt on the other. The bolt was of the spring variety, and when the windows were closed it automatically locked where the two sashes joined in the centre.

Up at the top and down at the bottom, respectively, there were bolts on the half of the window containing the catch, and these were at present pressed home. Thus for safety the window depended in reality on the one middle spring-catch, trusting to the bolting of the other sash to prevent the window being forced without considerable trouble.

What had caught Blake's eye, however, was the tiniest shred of cotton-wool hanging to the edge of the brass. So small was it that he held his breath lest it might be blown away, and quickly drawing a pair of fine tweezers from his pocket, he nipped it off and took it over to the desk.

There he laid it down and returned to the window.

Up and down the sash he worked on the inside until every particle had been covered. This finished and nothing else being discovered, he pressed back the bolt and stepped out on to the balcony.

"Ask the butler to bring a hand-light of some sort," he called to Carslake, who had followed him.

"Or, stay! Tinker, I believe, has his electric-torch with him. Just slip out into the hall and get it."

Carslake hurried away, and returned a moment later with Tinker's torch. Then Blake went to work on the low sill, which was almost flush with the balcony floor.

It was almost in the very middle of its edge that he once more bent, and a dry, hard glitter came into his eyes as he saw, caught in a splinter, another minute piece of cotton-wool. Again bringing the tweezers into requisition, he carefully disengaged it and re-entered the room. Laying it on the desk beside the other, he returned to the balcony.

Further along was a broad flight of steps leading to the terrace, but Blake disregarded these. Instead, he leaped lightly over the railing opposite the study window, landing on his toes on the soft turf below. Swinging the torch downwards, he dropped to his knees, and, like a human bloodhound, began nosing and working over the ground.

Owing to the thick carpet of grass, he had not many hopes of picking up a footprint, for grass has a habit of working back to the vertical after a foot has pressed it. However, he sought patiently for some part where the grass might be less thick, and near a supporting-post he found it.

In close against the edge of the balcony, and immediately under a spot where the rain-drip continually fell, the grass had not grown as thickly as elsewhere, and here he found the faint, curved edge of what could only be the impression of a foot.

True, it was more likely to be that of one of the gardeners than of anyone else; but since he had been searching for anything in the shape of a mark, and had finally found it, he would naturally follow it up.

Passing the torch up to the waiting Carslake, who stood leaning over, pulling nervously at his thin, light moustache, Blake nimbly vaulted back over the railing and landed softly.

"What's the next move?" inquired Carslake, following Blake through the French window into the study.

"I am going to try an experiment," replied Blake shortly. "Just wait where you are, please, until I call my assistant."

Going to the door and throwing it open, Blake called softly up the hall to Tinker, and signed for him to bring Pedro along to the study. A moment later the lad was at the door, whispering: "Found anything suspicious, guv'nor?"

Blake vouchsafed no answer, but taking Pedro's leash from Tinker, drew the lad inside and closed the door. Carslake meanwhile had partially closed the windows, and stood waiting with the torch in his hand for Blake's next move.

Whatever that was he was not to find out for a few moments, for barely had Pedro entered than Blake and Tinker watched with puzzled brows the dog's strange actions, while Carslake drew back startled. And well he might!

Pedro, one of the best-trained and most sagacious of bloodhounds, stood stock still where he had paused when Blake closed the door. But his appearance underwent a startling change. Suddenly, and without the slightest warning, every hair on his body stood out stiff and straight as a multitude of needles, his great ears went back angrily, his great jaws dropped threateningly, and he grew rigid as though cast in granite.

At first Blake thought it might be caused by the still, draped figure on the couch; but this he scouted almost at once, for Pedro had been in the presence of death too often to make such a to-do over it.

He bent forward and looked at the bloodhound's eyes, and gave a startled exclamation as he saw them. Like two fixed, blazing coals they returned his look unseeingly and without recognition.

If it is possible for animals to feel horror, then the expression in Pedro's eyes could only be described as that. Once in South America, Blake had seen a horse in mortal fear, and never to his dying day would he forget the look in the beast's eyes. They had held the same expression as Pedro's now held, together with the same fixed and rigid pose.

He began to straighten up, with the intent to speak sharply to the dog, when his words broke off, and all three were startled by a long, blood-freezing bay from the great hound.

Tinker, in a fever of anxiety as to what could be affecting Pedro so, dropped to one knee and endeavoured to pass an arm about the dog's neck; but Blake, suddenly springing forward, grasped him and dragged him back unceremoniously.

"Don't!" he whispered sharply. "Can't you see the dog is under a spell of horror? Carslake, come behind here where he can't see you — quick! Have the door open ready; and you, Tinker, stand near it. He is in such a state that he is not responsible. Quick!" he snapped; and Carslake barely reached safety as Pedro dashed madly forward as though filled with all the demons of the underworld.

Round and round the room he dashed, with Blake hanging desperately on to his collar. Then suddenly, as they passed close to the desk, Pedro pulled up suddenly, his lips bared, his teeth in an angry snarl, and with great red, dripping jaws, he launched himself straight at a large painting which hung over the desk.

Blake, strong as he was, had found it impossible to restrain him, and relaxed his hold as Pedro cleared the desk.

With a crash the big painting tumbled to the floor as Pedro struck it, and Blake leaped back as the dog turned.

A second later, however, he leaped forward and grasped the end of the leash as something shot past his head with a peculiar metallic rustle. A momentary silence had caused Pedro to hear that metallic sound, and, straight as an arrow, he shot after it. Blake, hanging on to the leash, went after him, but pulled hard as he saw the dog making for the window.

A moment later something struck the glass, rebounded, struck the sashes at the point where they were parted slightly owing to Carslake not having closed them tightly; then it disappeared.

So quickly had the whole thing happened that it was impossible for Blake to get an idea of the form of the thing which had flashed past him. That it was no larger than the end of his finger he felt positive, but that was all. With its disappearance Pedro tried to dash through the window after it, but Blake dragged hard on the leash and held him back.

As suddenly as he had apparently gone mad, did Pedro regain his usual condition. His hair grew flat, his eyes assumed their old expression, and his ears hung slackly; but no man there would ever forget the haunting sound of his blood-freezing bay of a few moments before. As for Carslake, he stood, white as chalk, where Blake had placed him, and Tinker hastened across to the dog.

Between them, Blake and the lad made a hurried examination of him, but he was as normal as ever, and, beyond a few flecks of foam on his jaws, showed no signs of the hurricane rage which had just possessed him.

Passing the leash to Tinker, Blake hastened across to the desk, and, moving around it, made an examination of the fallen picture. Suddenly he gave a muttered exclamation, and bent forward.

When he straightened up, he held in his hand a tiny ball of cotton-wool of a similar texture and colour to the two pieces he had found at the window. But one thing he noticed about it which he had failed to detect in the others, and that was a very faint perfume.

With a very thoughtful manner, Blake placed the piece of cotton-wool on the desk beside the other pieces, and then signing to Carslake to bring the torch, he took Pedro's leash from Tinker and led the way outside.

This time he passed along the balcony and down the steps, keeping along in the thick turf until he had reached the footprint which he had seen before. There he put Pedro at the impression, and after waiting patiently until the bloodhound had thoroughly got the scent, he eased the leash, and gave Pedro his head.

Close against the balcony hung Pedro until he reached the steps. There he turned, and crossed the gravelled path, taking again to the turf on the other side, and once more hugging the balcony.

Suddenly at the very end of the balcony, and at the base of a supporting pillar, he paused and sniffed upwards. In a moment Blake had signed to Tinker.

"Up you go, my lad!" he rapped. "Our quarry has gone up the post. I'll pass Pedro up to you."

As nimbly as a monkey, Tinker wrapped his legs about the post, and, given a starting boost from Carslake, he was soon drawing himself over the edge. As he knelt on his knees and leaned over, Blake picked Pedro up in his arms. Heaving the dog upwards, he held him while Tinker caught his collar. Then, with Pedro bracing his hind feet against the pillar, he drew up while Blake pushed, and, with a spring, Pedro landed safely.

"Let him follow it up there, and see where he goes," jerked Blake.

"All right, guv'nor," replied Tinker. "He's on it now!"

It was true Pedro was on it, but he took barely three steps before he stopped, worried.

"What's the trouble?" asked Blake irritably.

"I don't know, guv'nor. He has stopped about six inches from the end, and doesn't seem able to pick it up again."

"Walk about the top of the balcony, and see if he can get it again," ordered Blake.

With an "All right!" Tinker drew on the leash and began methodically pacing the length and breadth of the balcony. His efforts were of no avail, however, for beyond the one spot at the end of the balcony, Pedro seemed unable to get the scent. Tinker finally desisted, and returned to the edge.

"It's no use, guv'nor," he said. "He can't pick it up. It seems to have vanished into the air."

Blake grunted.

"Very well. Pass him down, and then come down yourself."

Tinker did so, and when they had landed safely, Blake took the electric-torch and extinguished it. With a muttered remark to the others to remain where they were, the detective moved back and gazed upwards.

Before him was the rear of Sir George's house, with the balcony running the full width. Behind him stretched the terraces and garden, while on either side rose high walls, separating the grounds where he stood from the adjoining gardens of the next-door houses.

Between each side of Sir George's house and the dividing walls there was a space of fully twenty feet, which, after a further glance round, Blake verified by pacing the distance.

It would have been easier to work by the assistance of the torch, but in view of the remarkable seizure which Pedro had had, and the finding of the third bit of cotton-wool, Blake was beginning to suspect that after all, there might be something very sinister behind everything.

Consequently, when the trail he had discovered ended so mysteriously, he preferred to be on the safe side by working in the light cast by the stars, rather than run the risk of having his movements watched by some unseen person.

Carslake watched him curiously, while even Tinker was puzzled by seeing his master pacing the distance between each side of the house and the dividing wall.

After he had paced out the distance, Blake stood back in the shadow of the balcony, under the spot where the trail had ended. For some moments he made no move, the while he searched with his eyes the shadowy bulk of the house on the other side of the wall. Not a single light gleamed in any of the rooms, and, turning to Carslake, he asked briefly: "Do you know if that house is occupied?"

"I don't know," responded the other. "You see, I don't know very much about the neighbourhood. Sir George only returned a week ago, and previous to that Miss Halliday was staying with her aunt."

"I see. However, it doesn't matter now. We will return to the library. But before doing so let me say a few words to you, to which I want you to pay the closest attention.

"In the first place, my discoveries, though very vague and very slight so far, have been sufficient to convince me that there is a strong probability — note, please, I only say probability — that Sir George did not die naturally, nor by his own hand. That being so, it is essential that his enemies, if such exist, must be kept in ignorance of the fact that foul play is suspected.

"To attain that end it will, in my opinion, be of the utmost importance to keep our suspicions secret for the time being. Until I feel more certain of my ground I don't care to make any explicit statements, and since he is dead, I think it best to permit things to go ahead for the present as though the death had been a natural one. Not even the old butler must know that we suspect anything."

"All right, Mr. Blake," replied Carslake. "I'll do exactly as you suggest. But how about Miss Halliday?"

"It would serve no useful purpose at present to tell her anything," replied Blake. "On the contrary, she is sufficiently upset already by the shock, and should it be necessary for me to gain any details by questioning her later, I will then tell her myself."

Carslake heaved a sigh of relief.

"I'll be jolly glad for you to take the responsibility." he said. "In the meantime, if there is anything I can do, command me. As for funds" — and he laughed apologetically — "well, I'm not exactly a pauper. If there has been any foul play I'd spend my last penny in order to run Sir George's murderers to earth."

"We will discuss that later," replied Blake. "For the present I will look after that part of it myself."

With that he turned and led the way back to the house where they found the doctor who had returned.

"Ah, Mr. Carslake," he said, "I was just looking for you."

"What can I do, doctor?" asked Carslake. "By the way, permit me to introduce you to a friend of mine, Mr. Smith."

He had just caught Blake's warning nudge in time, and stammered slightly as he mumbled over the name; but the fussy little doctor was too much taken up with his own importance to notice Carslake's momentary embarrassment.

"How do you do, sir?" he said hurriedly, as Blake bowed. Then, turning to Carslake, he went on: "I have made out the certificate — called it heart failure. I waited to see you though. I suppose you will look after the arrangements for the family?"

"Yes," replied Carslake gravely. "I have already sent for Miss Halliday's aunt, and will see about everything else for them."

"Then I will hurry along," answered the doctor. "Good-night! Good-night, Mr. Smith."

With a bow to Tinker, who stood just inside the window, he was gone.

At that moment the old butler entered to inform Carslake that by the doctor's orders they had removed Sir George to his bedroom upstairs, and then he informed them that he had prepared a meal, if they cared for it.

Carslake was too upset to eat anything, but Blake and Tinker had been through too many scenes of a similar nature to be affected in that manner. Consequently, both the lad and his master did justice to the food the old butler had prepared, while Carslake drank sparingly of a glass of wine.

Then, informing Carslake he would communicate with him on the morrow, Blake signed to Tinker, and, with Pedro following, the famous Baker Street trio took their departure.

They walked along for some distance before a taxi came in sight. Hailing it, they climbed in, and giving the address, Blake sank back and closed his eyes, while Tinker pulled Pedro's ears, and puzzled over the events of the evening, not least of which was the attack which had seized Pedro in the library.

The lad started slightly as Blake's voice suddenly broke the silence.

"Did you see the thing which went past me, and escaped through the narrow opening between the windows?" asked Blake.

"No, guv'nor," replied Tinker. "I heard it, though. It sounded like scales rubbing together, and made me creep."

"Quite so, my lad; but doesn't it occur to you to wonder at Pedro's attack?"

"Indeed, yes, guv'nor. I can't make it out."

"Nor can I, my lad; but this much is certain. While we were in the room there was something there of a sinister nature. We couldn't detect it, but in that mysterious way only known to animals, Pedro's canine intelligence detected it at once, and, my lad, he felt the horror of it. That is proof conclusive. Then, although he was rigid with fear, his natural bravery overcame that, and he attempted to locate it, and stamp it out. That was when I drew you back, for he could not recognise either you or myself. I had seen that in his eyes, and I never want to see them look that way again.

"With the escape of the thing, however, he immediately regained his usual condition; but, my lad — and mark well what I say — that thing which was so sinister as to upset Pedro, as it did, had some bearing on Sir George Halliday's death. I have seen many things tonight which, I must confess, puzzle me as much as I have ever been puzzled, but I feel positive the thing which escaped had some bearing on the cause of his death, and had it not been for Pedro we would hardly have seen it; or else, by some means, we may have followed in the footsteps of Sir George. But we will bring deduction to bear on it, my lad, and if I am not mistaken, it will need all our resources to ferret the thing out."

With this Blake closed his eyes again, and silence reigned once more until the taxi drew in to the kerb in Baker Street.

A moment later they were back in the consulting-room, and Blake was spreading out on the desk the varied assortment of articles which he had brought from Sir George's house, and which consisted of the following.

The blotting-pad, the sheet of paper on which Sir George had been writing, the pen he had used, together with the rest of the pens in the tray, a small bottle full of the ink from the stand, the blue pencil, a few plain envelopes and sheets of paper similar to that which the dead baronet had been using, and lastly the two tiny shreds and the larger piece of cotton-wool which he had found.

Little did Blake know as he bent over the articles, that outside stood a dark figure which had followed them the whole way from Sir George's house. And even had they known it, they would not have known that the figure had slipped forth after them from the front gate of the house adjoining Sir George's.

* * *

"Now, my lad, here is your programme for this morning."

It was the morning after the evening on which occurred the events related above. After their arrival at Baker Street, Blake had sent Tinker to bed, and with only Pedro keeping him company, he had spent many long hours examining the articles he had brought from Sir George Halliday's.

It was daylight when he retired, but after only a couple of hours' rest he was up again and at work. They had breakfasted in silence, for Tinker, reading the signs, offered no comments of any sort until Blake chose to speak. He had done so only when they had adjourned to the consulting room, and Tinker waited for him to go on.

"I want you," continued Blake, stuffing his pipe full of black tobacco, "I want you to disguise in something, and go along to where we were last night. Just walk past, and find out if the houses on either side are occupied. It will be easy enough to tell. If not, find out who the agents are. It is unlikely that both will be empty, if either, but I wish to know. If they are occupied, get into conversation with the policeman on the beat, and find out what you can about the tenants. They are large places, and require people with a fairish income to keep them up. Consequently, the officer should be able to tell you what you wish to know. As soon as you have found out what you can, return here at once."

"Very well, guv'nor," replied Tinker, making for his room in order to change. "I'll find out all I can. Will you be here when I return?"

"If I am not, wait until I come," replied Blake briefly; and with that he sank into the big chair, and began thoughtfully smoking.

At nine o'clock punctually, however, he stirred and rose. Tinker had been gone some time, but Blake evidently didn't propose to await his return, for he entered his dressing room, and emerged a moment later, wearing his hat and coat. Then speaking to Pedro, and telling him to look after things, Blake made his way to the street, and hailed a passing taxi.

Giving the address, 'The Chinese and Tibetan Research Society', Blake stepped into the cab, and leaned back with puckered brows. Twenty minutes later he was asking for the curator, Professor Somers, and when shown into that gentleman's office found him seated before a littered desk, an open letter in one hand, a crumpled newspaper in the other, and a blank look of startled amazement on his face.

"Ah, Professor Somers," remarked Blake, as he seated himself, and returned the professor's rather flurried greeting.

"I see you have read the sad news coincident with your receipt of Sir George's letter."

"Why, bless my soul!" gasped the bespectacled little man. "You are positively uncanny, Mr. Blake. How on earth did you know? What a very terrible thing it is!"

"It was very simple," replied Blake, smiling slightly. "I myself instructed the butler to post that letter, professor. It was written just a few minutes before his death. You are right. It is a very sad and very sudden affair."

"To think," cried the professor, "that Halliday of all men should die of heart failure. Why, hang it, he struck me as being as strong and vigorous as an ox. I can hardly believe it, for think of the altitudes to which he went in the Himalayas, Mr. Blake. No man with a weak heart could stand the cold and the rarity of that atmosphere. But perhaps it was the strain which really weakened his heart. Ah, yes, very sad — very sad! To think that I received a letter, too, written just before his death."

"Yes, it brings the thing home rather forcibly to you, professor," remarked Blake gravely; "but I took it upon myself to have that letter posted for a certain reason."

"Eh — what — er — I don't understand, Mr. Blake."

"For reasons sufficiently weighty, professor, I desire to read its contents. I realise my request is distinctly out of the ordinary, but I think you know me well enough to be aware that I would not make such a request unless I had a very strong motive."

"Why, as far as I know, Mr. Blake, I see no reason why you shouldn't read it. As you say, it is a bit irregular, but as we are — er — fellow scientists in a way, I have no objection. In fact, now I think of it, I am rather glad.

"I knew Sir George very intimately, but, to say the least, his letter struck me as rather peculiar. And then this awful shock of his death. Oh, dear — oh, dear, you really must excuse me, Mr. Blake."

The warm-hearted little professor blew his nose violently, and handed the letter to Blake, who walked with it to the window in order to give the professor time to recover from his emotion. There he read the letter, which ran as follows:

MY DEAR PROFESSOR SOMERS, — I am seizing the first opportunity since my return in order to write to you, knowing you will be keenly interested to hear what knowledge I have acquired on the subjects dear to your heart as well as to mine during my last trip.

Rest easy, old friend. I have a fund of notes with me which will satisfy even your insatiable appetite, and I foresee many interesting hours in the discussion and cataloguing of them. I will bring them with me at three in the afternoon on Friday, when you can arrange a schedule of days for their investigation.

In the meantime, professor, I should be greatly obliged if you would look carefully through your records and endeavour to find some trace of the following insect — or beetle — which I believe exists in China, and which I also have reason to believe is a mud borer. I have searched every book and record I have, but can discover no trace of it. Unfortunately I have no specimen, and can only give you a vague description. However, here it is.

In size I have an idea it is about that of the common bluebottle. As colour, I think, is yellow or yellowish. When flying and crawling, its wings make a peculiar metallic sound — not unlike scales being rubbed together — and in addition, I have strong reason to believe it has in front of its head a horn, or borer. Of the length of this I have no idea, and, in fact, am not certain that it really exists. Lastly, professor, it is of a deadly poisonous nature. This fact I am thoroughly certain of, and furthermore, know that its poison kills within a few seconds. I might add that it is very partial to a perfume of some description, but as to its nature I am ignorant.

You must pardon my speaking of this matter in my letter, and you will probably think it could have waited until I came myself.

It is, however, of an urgent nature, and I trust you will be able to find some record of the insect I have described.

Sincerely,
GEORGE HALLIDAY

Blake read the letter with great care, memorising in every detail the description of the beetle mentioned by Sir George. Then he turned and walked very thoughtfully back to the desk.

"Well, Mr. Blake," asked the professor, "what do you think of it?"

"I must confess that although I was not so intimately acquainted with Sir George as were you, professor, still I knew him fairly well, and must say I agree with you. I think it is a bit — er — peculiar shall I say?"

"That was exactly my impression!" assented the professor.

"By the way," went on Blake casually, "might I ask if you have any knowledge, professor, of any such bug or beetle as he describes?"

The professor placed the tips of his fingers together and pursed up his lips.

"Well, Mr. Blake, off-hand, I can't say I do. There are of course, a good many mud-borers, and, from what I remember, several would fulfil his description in one, or perhaps two, ways. At the moment, however, I have no recollection of any such as he describes. Of course, the list of poisonous beetles is not large, and unless it is of a species unknown so far, it shouldn't be hard to discover its identity. I have in mind a beetle which, so far, has only been found along the head waters of the Magdalena in Colombia; but, if my memory serves me correctly, it is black — inky-black — and consequently would not comply with the points mentioned by Sir George, which demand that it should be yellow or of that shade."

"Might it be possible that it would acquire that shade when shedding its skin?" suggested Blake.

"H'm — yes — possible!" replied the professor, with a rising inflection. "Yes, on consideration, Mr. Blake, that is a point worth looking into, and I will bear it in mind. It is, however, not probable!"

"I suppose, in any event, you will endeavour to look up such a beetle, won't you?" asked Blake.

"Certainly! Since it was an urgent wish of my poor friend, I shall do so at once. In fact, this very day I shall start, although the information will be of no use to him now."

"I'm not so sure, professor!" said Blake softly.

"Eh — ah! What?" asked the old man, starting up. "What do you mean, Mr. Blake?"

"Listen, professor," said Blake earnestly. "If I ask you to trust me for a few days, will you do so? All I can say at present is that any information you can give me on the subject of the beetle Sir George describes, may be of great use. If he could speak, I can assure you he would say so himself. Will you trust me, and for the present ask no

34

questions?"

As he finished, Blake looked at the professor with his rare, winning smile, and the old man nodded.

"Yes, Mr. Blake!" he said huskily. "I will. What do you wish me to do?"

"This, professor. I want you to start as soon as possible and look up what you can about this beetle. Everything, you understand? Its habits, its characteristics, and, in fact, all that pertains to it. Will you do this?"

"I will begin at once," answered the professor.

"Thank you!" said Blake. "If you find anything, will you send me a wire at once?"

And even as Blake opened the door, the old man was already beginning his search.

"He'll be a willing worker," muttered Blake, as he reached the street. "He is working for love of his friend, and no inspiration could be stronger."

Re-entering the taxi, Blake told the driver to proceed to the offices of Dodds, Milne & Co.

There he found the manager had received Sir George's letter, and although he demurred slightly at first, when Blake asked permission to read it, he finally capitulated.

It was merely an order for half a dozen books which Sir George requested should be sent at once, but, of course, the manager explained, on reading in the papers of his sudden death, he had naturally not sent them.

"Have you all these books in stock now?" asked Blake.

"Yes, certainly! We always carry a supply of every book in our catalogue."

Blake made no reply, but drew out his cheque-book and opened it. Then he spoke.

"I will take a copy of each," he said quietly. "I am under the impression I already have two of them in my library, but that doesn't matter."

The manager was unable to refrain from showing the astonishment he felt, but, as they were all exceptionally expensive books, he lost no time in giving orders for them to be packed up.

Twenty minutes later Blake entered the taxi bearing a parcel in his arms, which contained six books of a highly scientific nature, and with the following titles:

Insects, Flies and Beetles of India.

Insects of Japan.

Mud-boring Beetles of the World.

Tree-boring Beetles of the World.

Insects and Beetles of China and Tibet — (translated from the original).

Poisonous Beetles of the World — (a complete treatise, translated from the original).

Rather a formidable array; but Blake was nothing if not thorough, and hard as he knew the professor would work, he was determined to apply his own knowledge to the research.

On his arrival at Baker Street, he expected to find Tinker had returned. The lad, however, was nowhere to be seen, and instead, sitting nervously on the edge of a seat, was a poorly-clad woman with wan features, whose whole appearance spoke of poverty and the East End.

She rose and curtseyed to Blake as he entered, and then spoke in trembling tones. "Please, sir, are you Mr. Blake?"

Blake nodded.

"Yes," he said kindly, "I am Mr. Blake. Are you in trouble? If so, what can I do for you?"

"Oh, please, sir, I am sorry to take up your time, but I have been to two other men, sir, and they refuse to help me unless I pay them a lot of money, and, sir, I haven't a penny. I wouldn't have come to you, sir, with my troubles, but my married daughter insisted. She says as how you often help poor people who can't afford to pay."

"You are quite right, Mrs. —"

"Green, sir!"

"Thank you! As I was saying, Mrs. Green, you are quite right. Rich or poor, it makes no difference to me, but in order that my help be received free of charge, three things are necessary."

"What are they, please, sir?" asked the woman fearfully.

"One is, they must be worthy; the second that the trouble must be serious enough to demand my assistance; and the third, that they must be perfectly frank with me in every way. Do you think you can fulfd all those conditions?"

"Oh, yes, sir!" cried the poor soul. "I can indeed!"

"Very well," replied Blake, laying his books down with a

regretful sigh. "Tell me what is the trouble!"

"Please, sir, it is" — and her voice trembled — "like the end of the world to me. My son — my only son Tom — him as was stoker on a ship between here and Chiney is dead, sir, and I can't believe it is heart failure, which the doctor says it is. He was so hale and hearty, sir, and I haven't liked the looks of those foreign devils — begging your pardon, sir — as has been hanging around the neighbourhood ever since he arrived home three weeks ago."

"Just what do you mean by 'foreign devils'?" asked Blake quietly.

"Heathen, sir — Chinamen; but not like the laundryman at the corner, sir."

"And you think your son's death is due to them?" asked Blake quickly, as he rose and began walking up and down.

"Yes, sir; I do. I can't believe my Tom's heart was weak."

"Wait, wait, Mrs. Green!" said Blake suddenly, and holding up his hand. "I wish to scribble a note, and then I will come with you to your home."

Five minutes later, after writing a note to Tinker, Blake was in a taxi with Mrs. Green beside him, speeding eastwards on a mission which was to increase the mystery of the baffling maze in which he seemed to be entering.

[Overleaf image is from a 1940 version of the same story in *Detective Weekly*. /drf]

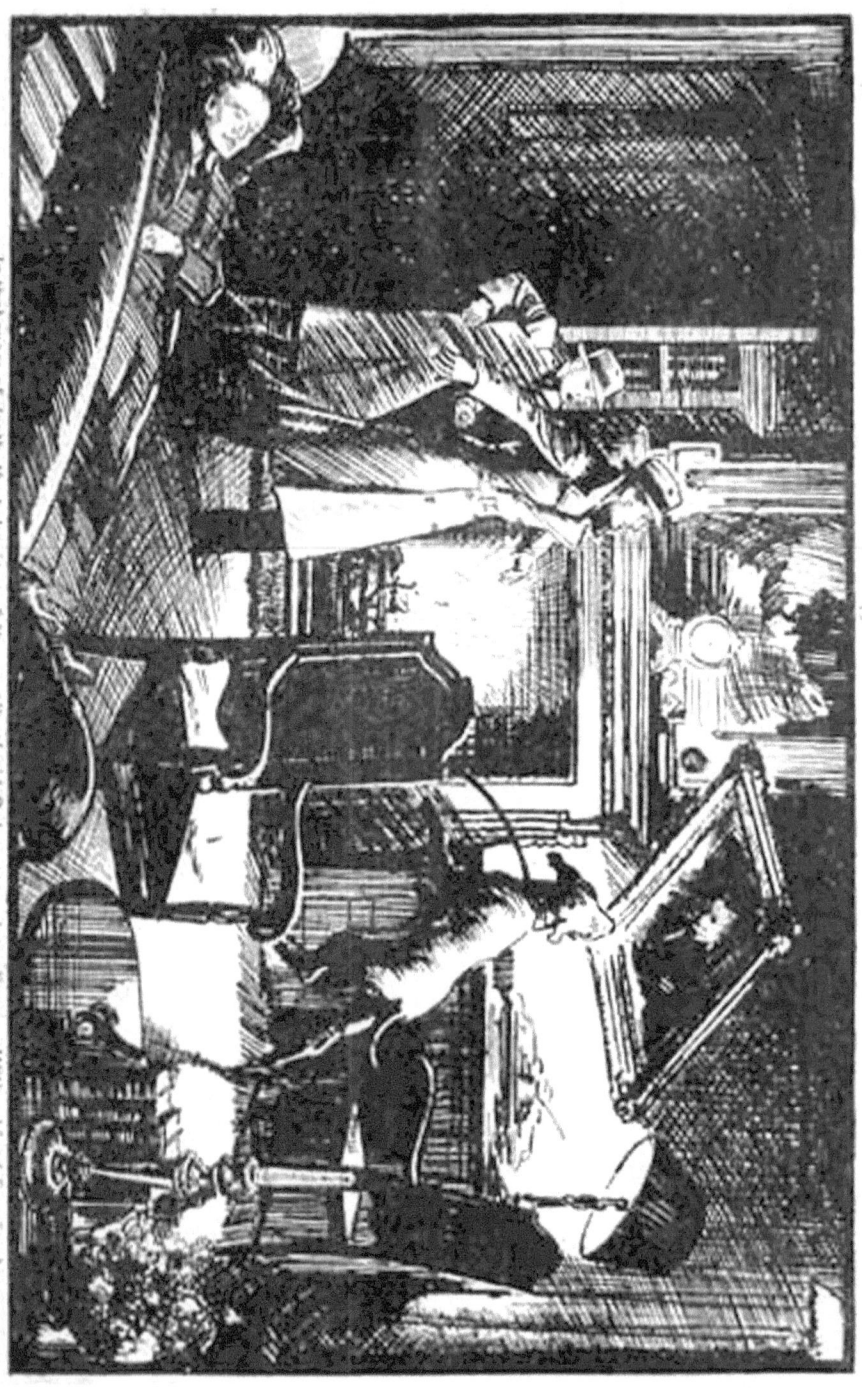

CHAPTER III. Tinker Reconnoitres — The Trap that Failed — The Struggle at Baker Street — Pedro on Guard

When Tinker was sent by Blake to disguise himself and proceed to make investigations in the neighbourhood of the late Sir George Halliday's house, he chose, as he had often done before, the suit which gave him the appearance of a ragged Italian boy. When he had donned this and brought into play his knowledge of the language, he made such a perfect representation of the part that more than once he had befooled native Italians themselves.

It came in particularly useful in the crowded precincts of Soho, but experience had taught him it was equally useful in the West End. Consequently, when he slipped quietly through the consulting-room and gained the street, he thought, as he breathed in a deep breath of the fresh morning air, that he was thoroughly safe from discovery, should any risk arise.

Although Blake was beginning to feel vaguely the force of a mysterious and sinister power behind the cause of Sir George's death, he was as yet in a maze of threads, each one of which seemed to be inextricably tangled up with the others.

His deductions from an analysis of the strange occurrences which had taken place, plus the mystifying letter written by Sir George to Professor Somers, made him certain that the baronet had not died by natural means.

Still, that was as yet only a tentative hypothesis, all he had on which to build it being an extremely minute mark on Sir George's lower lip, and the thing which had caused Pedro's strange actions in the library.

Part of this, however, he only found out during the morning when he went to see the professor, and with his master still knowing so little, Tinker knew even less, for Blake had confided nothing to him since the conversation in the cab the previous night on their way home.

Consequently, neither he nor Blake had been aware of the figure which had followed them home, and had stood on guard throughout the night. Nor did they know that, when Tinker issued forth, the same figure swung along after him at a safe distance.

Tinker hailed the first taxi he saw, and, grinning to himself as the driver seemed inclined to doubt his ability to pay for it, he climbed in and spoke in extremely plain English.

"Look alive, fathead!" he said pleasantly. "Haven't you learned yet that things are not always what they seem?"

"What in blazes do you mean by talking first in a Dago lingo that I can't understand?" grumbled the driver. "What are you masquerading in them things for?"

"Would you really like to know?" asked Tinker. "Because if you would, I don't mind telling you. But first I must swear you not to breathe it to a soul. The fact is the German Emperor is arriving today, and I am on the reception committee. And now send me along Piccadilly, fathead!"

Tinker slammed the door as the driver turned back to his wheel with a sheepish smile.

The short colloquy was an unfortunate delay for Tinker, however, for it gave the man following him sufficient time to secure a taxi and continue his surveillance of Tinker's movements.

Had the lad been able to see the narrow, deep-set, almond eyes which followed his course, he would have felt something akin to the sensation which had caused Pedro to fly into such a rage the previous night. He knew it not, however, and whistled blithely to himself as the cab threaded its way up Piccadilly.

At Hyde Park Corner Tinker descended, and, after some further chaff with the driver, sauntered along until he reached the street where Sir George's house was situated.

It was in the form of a crescent, and completely lined with big houses, thus making it impossible to see very far along it before the curve cut off the view. Half way along, and just as he was approaching Sir George's house, he caught sight of a policeman coming towards him.

As he drew near he glanced suspiciously at Tinker, and made as though to question him.

Tinker, however, greeted the officer familiarly.

"Hallo, Kelly!" he said cheerily. "You are the very man I'm looking for."

"Well, I'm blest!" grinned the big officer, as he recognised Tinker's voice. "I was just debating whether or not to ask what a ragged individual like you wanted up here. What's on? Nothing wrong in this neighbourhood, is there?"

"Oh, no," replied Tinker. "I'm just out after a little information which perhaps you can give me."

"Well?" inquired Kelly. "Go ahead! If it's anything on my beat I can probably tell you what you want to know."

"Thanks!" said Tinker. "You see that house over there — Sir George Halliday's?"

"Yes; but why do you ask? He died last night."

"I know, Kelly. I don't want to know anything about it, but I do want to know what you can tell me about the tenants of the houses on either side of it. I see they are both occupied."

"Well, I'm afraid I can't tell you very much," replied Kelly, sweeping the street with his eyes, and thrusting his thumbs in his belt. "Mr. Fordham, the financier, lives in one of them, but the other has only been occupied for about a fortnight. Foreigners have taken it. Chinese they are, and I imagine from their looks they are mighty high caste. They have all Chinese servants, too, so I haven't found out much about them."

"You say they have only been there for about a fortnight?" remarked Tinker thoughtfully.

"Yes. They arrived on a Saturday, for I remember it was wet. They have leased the place furnished, and must have paid a pretty figure, for it really belongs to Colonel Porter, who himself returned about the same time. He is gone to a private hotel to live, and you can bet he wouldn't do that unless they made it worth his while. However, Tinker, if I'm not mistaken, you will have a chance to see one of them now. See that big limousine coming up the street?"

Tinker nodded.

"They keep that in a garage in the rear, and it's not the only one they have got. You will see one of them come out in a few minutes."

"Crikey!" muttered Tinker. "I wonder what I'd better do. I'll wager the guv'nor never expected the house was occupied by Chinamen, and that they had only been in it a fortnight. It's a toss-up whether to go back and report at once, or to follow that limousine."

His musings were interrupted by a nudge from Kelly.

"Look! Quick, Tinker! There is the chap who lives there! Isn't he swell stuff?"

Tinker looked up, and saw descending the steps a tall, grave-looking Chinaman. He knew enough of that race to know that the man was a pure Manchu, and from his undoubted wealth and the dignity of his carriage, evidently an important personage.

The man driving the limousine, as well as the footman, were also Celestials, and the marked obsequiousness of their manner only convinced Tinker all the more that the master was a personage.

"You don't know his name, do you?" he asked of Kelly.

"No. I did hear it, but those Chinese names are such jaw-breakers. I call them all "John"!"

At that moment the man across the street entered the limousine, and very slowly it began moving along.

Tinker, with a muttered word to Kelly, swung round and started after it, keeping a sharp eye open the while for a taxi.

Had he known of the man who had followed him, and had he also known that as soon as he saw Tinker enter the crescent he had hurried along the lane at the back of Sir George's house and then into the house in which Tinker was interested, and furthermore that the departure from the house of the man in the limousine was firstly and lastly solely on Tinker's account, the lad would have thought twice before he started after the slowly-moving motor. On the contrary, he would have gone as fast as a taxi could take him to Baker Street, and there reported to his master what he had seen, for of a surety it would need a Blake, and all the subtlety of a Blake, to combat the force which was beginning its work of terror in England.

Ignorant of this fact, and keen to acquire as much knowledge as he could regarding the inhabitants of the house next to Sir George's, Tinker hailed the first taxi he saw, and told the driver to follow the limousine ahead.

There was certainly no trouble in keeping it in sight, for it continued to move at only a moderate pace. When they had been winding through the traffic for some time, Tinker finally saw that the car ahead was going steadily towards the East End of the City, and, like a flash, he muttered "Limehouse!"

Although the almond-eyed man following Tinker had for many hours successfully kept up his surveillance without being discovered, it was not an easy matter to keep either Blake or Tinker shadowed continually without their dropping to it.

Like the criminals they hunt, a detective must keep his eyes open to each side, and behind as well as in front, and although stress of matters had kept Tinker completely engaged in watching the car ahead, as they entered the purlieus of Limehouse, he cast his eyes through the little window at the back of the taxi.

Catching sight of the taxi behind, it for the moment created no suspicion in his mind; but when after taking many devious turns, it still followed at the same distance, it suddenly dawned to Tinker that he was being followed.

"Well, crikey!" he muttered. "I wonder how long that taxi has been following me? It must have been on my trail ever since I started after the heathen ahead, and, perhaps, even longer. There's more in the thing than I thought; but I'll bet even the guv'nor didn't know we were being watched. I'd give something to know where that limousine is going; but it's no use. I'll have to shake off this chap behind, and get back to Baker Street."

With that Tinker picked up the speaking-tube which, for a wonder, was in working order, and as soon as he had attracted the driver's attention, gave him his instructions.

The man nodded, and kept on until they reached a corner. There, taking advantage of the extra space, he suddenly turned in a sharp swing, and headed back exactly as he had come.

Just as they were getting up speed again the other taxi swept by them, and Tinker got a fleeting glimpse of a pair of dark, sinister-looking eyes. He hurriedly looked back, but instead of following him the other taxi put on more speed, and Tinker's brow clouded.

"That means," he muttered, "that the man in the taxi following me is putting on speed in order to get in touch with the man in the limousine; but my shadow was a Chinese, too. I wonder what their game was? Anyway, I'll not run any chances. I'll have my driver take me by a roundabout way in order to be sure I have shaken them off, and then I'll get back and report to the guv'nor."

Following out this decision Tinker once more got in touch with the driver, who put on all the speed he dared, and began a series of bewildering spurts and turnings which would have shaken off Sexton Blake himself.

Then, after half an hour of this, he swung back Citywards and headed for Baker Street.

Tinker paid him, and hurriedly ran up the steps in order to lose no time in making a report to his master; but even as he turned the handle of the consulting-room door he heard a scuffling noise within, accompanied by Pedro's angry growl.

Hastily throwing open the door Tinker stood on the threshold, and looked in amazement at the scene which presented itself.

Standing before the door opening into Blake's dressing-room was Pedro, his lips drawn back in an angry snarl, while crawling before him with a crooked-bladed knife in his hand was the immaculately-dressed high-caste Chinaman whom Tinker had followed to Limehouse.

How on earth he had managed to reach Baker Street so soon was a mystery to Tinker, nor did he have any time to wonder.

With a panther-like spring the crouching Celestial gained his feet and swung on Tinker. Without the slightest warning he followed up this spring by rushing precipitately at the lad.

Tinker had no time in which to pick up a weapon of defence. He reproached himself for having gone out without his revolver, which oversight now left him weaponless. He ducked sharply, however, as the Chinaman lunged fiercely, and, as the sharp point stuck in the door, Tinker dived for his assailant's knees. Tackling them in a strong grip, he heaved just as Pedro landed heavily on top of the Chinaman from a magnificent spring which had carried him clear over from the dressing-room door.

The Celestial, who was really Wu Ling himself, although Tinker did not then know it, began cursing rapidly in Chinese as Pedro landed. The sudden turn of events, however, seemed to endow him with the force of three men. With a violent wrench he threw Tinker free, ramming his head sharply between the lad's eyes as he did so.

Then he swung on Pedro, and, regardless of the dog's gaping jaws and powerful legs, he grappled with him. His strong, supple hands sank into Pedro's neck, and with a knowledge born of much experience, he insinuated his fingers around Pedro's windpipe.

Nobly as he struggled the dog was no match for Wu Ling, master of every subtlety of the East. Slowly the great bloodhound's head went back until Wu Ling was able to get an arm-lock under his jaw.

Tinker was lying helplessly dazed on the floor, and for the moment was *hors-de-combat.*

Wu Ling took no chance of his recovery, however, for, as soon as he had secured a powerful lock under Pedro's jaw he bent quickly, seized the dog by the hind legs, heaved upwards, and swung with all his strength, sending Pedro crashing through the half-open door of the dressing-room.

Then, glancing hurriedly at Tinker, Wu Ling pulled the knife from where it stuck in the door. He raised it, and made as though to hurl it at the prostrate lad; but a grey flash came flying from the dressing-room, and he turned sharply. Leaping for the door he slipped through and slammed it, just as Pedro, mad with rage, landed heavily against it.

Tinker stirred and sat up, and the first sound which met his awakening senses was the sharp slamming of the front door. The noise brought him to his feet, still dazed, but with a full realisation of what had happened.

Throwing open the door of the consulting-room he dashed along, and out to the street. His late antagonist, however, was nowhere to be seen, and even as he stood on the kerb Tinker saw the luxurious limousine swing into Baker Street from a side street and disappear rapidly in the distance.

He slowly made his way back to the consulting-room, and there rapidly ran his hands over Pedro. The big fellow was tough and strong, however, and beyond the shock of his fall had not suffered materially from his aerial journey through the door of the dressing-room.

To say the least, Tinker was savage, and he grew still more so when he thought over the events of the morning.

"I'll bet anything," he muttered, as he surveyed the disordered room, "that that bunch of Chinese had me shadowed while I was talking to Kelly. What a fathead I was not to be more careful! And then after spending half an hour in an elaborate attempt to shake off the taxi which was following me, I got home here just in time to find the Chinaman of the limousine in here.

"I wonder just what the guv'nor's idea was in sending me to find out who lived there. It's a dead cert, that they are on to me anyway; but have they any connection with Sir George Halliday's death, and if so, does the guv'nor suspect that? It beats me what that fellow wanted here. I'll just ferret around and see if he has touched anything; but I guess old Pedro prevented that. Crikey, he did go for me like a whirlwind!"

Tinker proceeded at once to make a hurried examination of the consulting-room, but nothing had been disturbed, and he concluded his thought had been correct. Pedro had prevented the visitor from carrying out his purpose, whatever that was.

During his examination, however, Tinker saw Blake's note which told the lad his master was gone to the East End, and expected to return by four or five in the afternoon. It was now past one, and as he stood holding Blake's note in his hand, Tinker decided he would utilise the remaining time which would ensue before Blake's return, in an effort to find out more of the mysterious occupants of the house next to Sir George's.

But first, in case he should be late, he would write a report of what had happened, and leave it for Blake. He seated himself at the desk, and began writing quickly.

"Guv'nor," he wrote, "am giving below my report, and am off again to make further investigations."

Then followed a minute description of his movements during the morning, ending with the surprise attack he had received on his arrival home.

"I'm sorry the Chinaman got away [he then wrote], but I can describe him to you. Anyway, there is a piece of his jacket left, which came away in Pedro's jaws. What he wanted here I don't know, but hope to be able to report more when I return.

"You may know the reason of his visit. This much is certain. Whoever is living in that house they are a hot bunch, and for some reason they have it in for us.

"TINKER"

Folding the note and sealing it, the lad stuck it in the interior of an odd-looking Japanese idol which was on the mantel. Then, turning the idol's face to the wall, in order to indicate to Blake that there was a note for him, Tinker rapidly changed his ragged disguise for one of a fashionable description, and, calling Pedro, snapped the leash on him and started out.

He moved with a greater degree of caution this time, and, in case he were being shadowed, he had cooked up a plan which he thought would fool anyone who was following him.

He hailed a taxi, and telling the chauffeur to drive first to Soho, he stopped at a disreputable-looking dwelling-house.

Then he descended, and with Pedro at his heels, entered the house. A tired-looking woman was fashioning paper flowers at a table, while a boy of about Tinker's size was arranging the finished flowers in several baskets preparatory to going out with them on the streets.

They greeted Tinker cordially, for more than once had the lad befriended them.

"I see you are going out, Tim," he said, after greeting the woman.

"Yes, sir!" replied the boy. "I did pretty well this morning, and thought I'd try the West End this afternoon. But can I do anything for you, sir?"

"Yes, Tim," smiled Tinker. "It won't take you long, I want you to take Pedro and enter that taxi outside. Tell the driver to take you to Baker Street, and get out there. Here is my key. Open the door and go into the consulting room. You remember how to get there?"

"Oh, yes, sir!"

"Very well! All you have to do is to sit there for half-an-hour. Then leave Pedro, put my key on the desk, and return home. Will you do that?"

"With pleasure, sir. I'll do everything exactly as you have told me."

"Good!" replied Tinker, laying a half-sovereign on the table. "You can keep that for your trouble, Tim. There may be people shadowing my movements, and when you go out with Pedro they will think it is I, and that I only stopped here in order to disguise myself."

"I understand, sir. I'll keep my head down and go right along."

A moment later, leading Pedro, Tim had disappeared, and Tinker turned to Mrs. Williams, Tim's mother.

"There is a back way out of here, isn't there?" he asked.

"Oh, yes, sir. It takes you out into a narrow alley, and if you go along to the end of it, then turn to the left, it brings you out into the Tottenham Court Road."

"Good! I'll go that way," replied Tinker.

Mrs. Williams showed him the way, and once he had gained the alley he swung along at a brisk pace.

In Tottenham Court Road Tinker caught the first taxi he saw, and giving as the address the crescent on which was situated Sir George Halliday's house, he lay back.

As the cab drew in before the house, which had the blinds drawn, Tinker knew his call would not cause any comment, for since the baronet's sudden death the night before many old friends had called to offer their condolences to his daughter.

Just before leaving the cab Tinker took the precaution to fix a jaunty little moustache on his upper lip, and after dismissing the taxi, walked with sober dignity up the steps.

The sorrowing old butler opened the door, and without any preamble Tinker stepped inside.

"You remember me, don't you?" he said, removing the moustache.

"Oh, yes, sir!" replied the butler, "now I do. Did you wish to make any further examination of the study, sir?"

"No! But what I wish is to pass through the house into the garden at the rear. I want to make an examination of the grounds by daylight. Do you mind?"

"Certainly not, sir. Miss Halliday is lying down, but I know she wouldn't mind. Tell me, please, sir, do you suspect anything unnatural about the master's death?"

Tinker, remembering Blake's caution to Carslake of the previous night, shook his head.

"I know absolutely nothing," he replied, and with a sorrowful shake of the head the old butler led the way through the hall to the study, wondering why, if nothing were wrong, his caller desired to make an inspection of the garden.

However, he was too well-trained to ask any farther question when Tinker had shown so plainly that he had nothing to tell him. The faithful old fellow would worry his mind and wonder, but for the present Tinker knew Blake's orders on that score must be obeyed.

He stood on the terrace and surveyed the tangled garden before him until the butler had gone back to the house. Far down against the wall dividing the garden from that of the house occupied by the Chinese was a small tool-house, the flat, sloping roof of which was a few inches below the top of the dividing wall. At one end, and almost covering the roof with its branches, was a thickly-leaved tree, and as soon as he cast his eyes on it Tinker gave a grunt of satisfaction.

"Couldn't be better," he muttered. "I'll lose no time in getting up there. It ought to overlook the whole place!"

Quickly he dived along the terrace until he reached the wall, and then, keeping in its shelter he made his way down the garden until he reached the tool-house.

He reconnoitred a bit, looking for a method of ascent. Nothing presented itself but the sill of the window, and he discovered that by gripping the edge of the roof he could just make it.

A spring carried him up, and pulling himself over the edge, he lay flat, squirming along slowly in order not to make any noise on the galvanised material of which the roof was composed. A disappointment met him when he reached the wall and lifted himself to peer over.

As he had thought, from his position he could overlook every inch of the next garden, but the branches screened him far less than he had imagined they would when looking at them from the ground.

Dropping back, he gazed up at the tangled branches overhead, some of which hung over the wall into the next garden.

Suiting the action to the word, Tinker raised himself cautiously and caught hold of an overhanging branch. Then he swung clear of the roof and landed with his feet on a branch lower down.

To a lad of Tinker's activity and training the ascent was child's play, and when he had gained a higher position he settled himself and breathed a sigh of satisfaction.

"This is splendid," he said to himself. "Couldn't be better. Now, Mr. Chinaman, we'll keep a watch on your place until five o'clock."

Tinker hardly hoped for anything of a decisive nature to occur, particularly during the afternoon, but he was more keen than ever to know all he could about the curious people who lived in the house on the other side of the wall, and at the same time to discover, if possible, the reason of the mysterious occurrence in the consulting-room a little before.

For over an hour he sat motionless, watching intently, but nothing of the slightest description occurred.

At the end of that time, however, the gate at the end of the garden which gave on to the lane, flew open, and the big limousine he had seen earlier in the day rolled in and entered the garage.

A minute later he saw the Chinaman with whom he had had the struggle in the consulting-room come out of the garage and walk slowly up a garden path towards the house. Almost simultaneously a rear door in the house opened, and another Chinaman, dressed in Oriental fashion, hurried down the path, and Tinker saw with a quiver of joy that the two Celestials would meet almost under the tree in which he sat.

He held his breath as the two Chinamen drew nearer and nearer, and finally met not ten feet from him.

He noticed at once the obsequiousness of the greeting which the man from the house gave the newcomer, but as to what they were saying Tinker could not distinguish. He knew some Chinese words, but so rapidly and earnestly was the conversation being carried on that he could glean nothing which sounded familiar.

The pantomime of the man who had arrived in the limousine, however, told him as plainly as could any words what was the subject of their conversation. He went through a vivid reproduction of what Tinker knew was the fight in the consulting-room, all the time keeping up a guttural flow of words.

Suddenly one word in English, spoken by the man who was obviously the master, caught Tinker's ears.

It was 'Blake', and it took little deduction to know that the fierce tones which accompanied the name boded ill for the detective.

Tinker bent eagerly forward in order not to miss anything, and to stamp indelibly on his mind the appearance of the two Celestials, when an awful thing occurred.

In his eagerness he leaned too far for the support of the branch on which he was resting. As his full weight came on the weak part it bent dangerously, and Tinker, with a smothered gasp, reached wildly for a branch above.

His efforts were too late, however, and with a slithering, slipping scramble he dived headlong, falling with a heavy thud at the feet of the two men standing beneath.

CHAPTER IV.   The Plot Thickens — The Puzzling Sketches — The Night of Horror — Another Bolt from the Blue

On his arrival at Mrs. Green's modest home, which he discovered was on the outskirts of Limehouse, Blake wasted no time in beginning his investigations. In the course of his long career he had had hundreds of people — yes, thousands — come to him with their troubles. No matter whether they could defray his expenses or not, Blake never refused a needy man or woman; but, as he told Mrs. Green, they must first prove that his assistance was really essential.

He had read honest trouble, and the sorrow of a heart-broken mother, in the poor woman's eyes, and even had she not mentioned her belief that her son had in some way fallen foul of some Celestials, Blake would have lent his aid.

He would, however, have delayed his trip until the evening, and instead, spent the afternoon poring over the books which he had procured from the publishers, Milne, Dodds & Co. For out of the class of facts which investigation had grudgingly supplied, and which his own brilliant analytical capacity had added to and elaborated, he was beginning to evolve a few concrete facts.

It was plain to him after his perusal of Sir George's letter to Professor Somers, that the peril of which the dead man had spoken to Carslake had been no chimera. Every word, every letter of the communication had breathed — in view of what had ultimately occurred — the urgent desire of a brave man to know exactly what he had to fight against. Much as Sir George knew — and Blake felt a very great deal of knowledge had gone with him — he had not been able to estimate at its full value the force which was working against him, and which had so well succeeded in striking him down. Putting two and two together, Blake decided that the beetle, regarding which Sir George had written to the professor, had played a leading part in the ultimate end of the drama.

He thought grimly of the description in the letter. Sir George had been vague and uncertain about most of the particulars regarding it, but of one thing he had been positive — deadly positive. He had known the sting of the beetle was fatal, and instantly so. That argued a definite knowledge of the beetle's power, but also proved that he had not been permitted to investigate the matter thoroughly.

And then again, his letter had been written to the professor on

Tuesday evening. He had made a definite appointment to see the professor on Friday afternoon. Why, then, had he asked the professor so urgently to look up such a beetle as he described, unless he felt himself in deadly peril?

Then again he had refused to permit the announcement of an engagement between his daughter and Carslake, until he had told Carslake of some peril which was hanging over him. Blake had known Sir George intimately enough to know that he was no panic-monger. On the contrary, the man's whole life had been one of dignity and quiet bravery.

"No!" he concluded. "If Sir George felt the peril was real, it must have been real, and in fact the baronet's death routed any doubt on that point."

Blake felt that his death had not been a natural one, and, moreover, though tentatively he felt convinced that the mysterious beetle of which Sir George had written had been the chosen instrument of his death, Blake did not yet go so far as to conclude the repulsive thing which had stirred Pedro to such depths, and which had escaped through the window, was the beetle, or being, that was the one chosen as the instrument.

Knowing so little of the mysterious insect, he took into account the fact that several might have been necessary in order that the blow should be certain. He had hoped for much from his examination of the bits of cotton-wool he had found, but before he had been able definitely to classify the perfume with which they had been saturated, it had all evaporated. Another proof that traces would not be plentiful.

The question first to be solved was, supposing Sir George to have met with foul play, and again, supposing the mysterious beetle to be part of the whole of the cause, who were behind it? Blake had not reached the definite point even yet, where he felt certain Celestials were engineering matters; but certainly Sir George had just returned from China, and everything so far pointed to the genesis of his peril in China.

The only connection which seemed to exist between the sudden death of a poor stoker in the East End, and the equally sudden death of a wealthy and distinguished baronet in the West End was, to Blake's mind, comprised in three facts. One was that both men had apparently died of heart failure while in perfect health; the second was that both men had just returned from the East; and the third, that vaguely in one, and positively in the other, native Chinese had apparently been connected.

Little enough to go upon truly, but Blake was beginning to realise that he was feeling the first shafts of a very powerful, a very subtle, and a very far-reaching power, and it behoved him to leave no stone unturned, in order to discover definitely just what that power was. Knowing that fact, he could fight it, but, not knowing it, like the ill-fated baronet, he might fall a victim within its toils.

It is unnecessary to give a detailed description of Blake's examination of Tom Green, who lay in the little room upstairs. Those who have followed the methods of Sexton Blake will be familiar with his mode of procedure. Sufficient is it to say that when he returned to the little kitchen where Mrs. Green sat weeping silently — the truly sorrowing are usually silent in their grief — he wore a very grave expression on his face. Above all, the hard, dry glitter of his eyes was particularly marked.

Only when greatly disturbed, or when coming to grips with one of his numerous foes, did that glitter assume a place in the detective's eyes. For the net result of his examination had coincided with the doctor's decree of heart failure, except in one thing. That one thing was a tiny spot on Tom Green's throat just where he buttoned his shirt.

The spot was of yellow, and rimmed by the yellow was a tiny black puncture in the very centre. That was all, but to Blake it held an immensity of meaning. Size for size, point for point, colour for colour, it was the fellow in every way of the spot he had seen on Sir George's lower lip.

Stepping gravely across the narrow width of the kitchen, Blake laid his hand on the sorrowing mother's shoulder.

"I fully realise you have much to sorrow for, Mrs. Green," he said gently, as for a moment the glitter disappeared from his eyes. "But what is done is done, and we poor mortals must accept the decree. It is, however" — and Blake's face looked strangely gaunt in the afternoon light, while the glitter returned once more to the deep-set eyes — "it is, however, in our power to justly avenge the wrongs done to us."

The poor woman lifted her tear-stained face, and looked up at him.

"Then — then, Mr. Blake, you think they have done my Tom

foul?"

"Mrs. Green," said Blake, in the same gentle tones, "why did you come to me to help you?"

"Because I trusted you as a true, honourable gentleman, sir."

"Then I want you to trust me still further," replied Blake. "All I can tell you at present is that your son, Tom — and I doubt not that he was a good son — is the victim of some force which as yet I have not defined. You are not the only sufferer, Mrs. Green. At this very moment at the other end of the city there is a poor, motherless girl, brought up in the lap of luxury, who is lying with an aching heart because, through the same fiendish mechanism, she has lost that which is dear to her — her father."

"I know I must accept what comes, Mr. Blake," answered the poor woman chokingly; "but it is hard. Tom was my all."

"You must try to bear up, Mrs. Green," said Blake; "and in the meantime, help me as much as you can in discovering the truth."

"I will, sir —I will!" she cried, her eyes flashing. "If you can discover them as has done for my Tom I'll do anything to help."

"It will only be necessary for you to answer me a few questions," answered Blake. "Tell me, first, how long was your son home?"

"Going on three weeks, sir!"

"Ah! And he was stoker in a ship which came from—"

"Chiney, sir. I don't just remember the name of the port."

"That is immaterial," replied Blake. "He came from China. Another question, Mrs. Green. Did he show any signs of worry since he arrived, or did he act quite as usual?"

"It's funny you ask me that, sir, because he was as glum as you please, sir, ever since he got home. I often thinks, sir, he felt something hanging over him."

"He was glum," repeated Blake. And then to himself, "Fact two." Aloud he said: "I am sorry to touch on this, Mrs. Green, but believe me, it is essential. Did he leave any papers of any particular description?"

"Only his insurance, sir. He was a good son, and as regards money, sir, I never need worry as long as I live. He spent a good deal of his earnings in that. But in there is something which might be of interest to you, though I don't think so."

"What is that?" asked Blake.

"Well, sir, Tom, he never showed any leaning, as it were, to drawing. Since he come home, though, sir, he drawed and drawed almost continually. I never seen him do that before."

"What were the subjects of his drawings?" asked Blake.

"They was all the same thing, sir — a spidery-looking animal what made me creep."

For once in his life, Blake's composure almost deserted him. Leaning forward tensely, he said: "Are there any of his drawings left?"

"Oh, yes, sir! The drawer in the kitchen table over there is half full of them."

"May I see them?"

"Yes, sir, of course."

With that, Mrs. Green rose, and walked over to the table. Pulling out the drawer she drew out a pile of papers, and walking back to Blake, handed them to him.

Without comment Blake took them, and spread them out on the table before him. For a moment the most prominent thing in his face was the hard glitter of the eyes. Then his lids fell as he leaned over the papers, and silence reigned.

One paper was the same as the other. Each and every one of them had a crude, rough drawing upon it, and it is not surprising that, to Mrs. Green, they were only 'spidery things'. To Blake, however, they were of the utmost importance. Some were large, some were small, but all were roughly alike, and conspicuous about all was the crude attempt to make them assume a beetle-like shape.

There were the bent, fragile legs, the flat head, a rough attempt to show the scaly wings; but, chief of all, on every one of them was a horn or needle-like point protruding from the head. By the aid of a cheap yellow crayon the drawings had been shaded yellow, and even as he looked at them Blake kept muttering to himself: 'The Yellow Beetle! The Yellow Beetle!'

Finally, he raised his head and said: "Do you mind if I keep these, Mrs. Green?"

"No, sir. As I said, anything I can do I will do. If those are of use to you keep them. Though, please, sir, when you finish with them, can I have them back? They were the last things he did, sir."

"Certainly," answered Blake. "I promise you I will take care of them and return them, I hope, soon. Now, another question or two, Mrs. Green. Where did your son have his laundry done, or did you do it for him?"

"I did his collars, sir, but his boiled shirts he had done at the laundry down the road."

"Ah, what kind of a laundry is it?"

"A Chinese laundry, sir. It's just two blocks down."

"He always had it done there, did he?"

"Oh, yes, sir! Though those laundry-men are always changing, sir."

"H'm! When did he receive his shirts home?"

"Well, sir, he always called for them Saturday night, but last Saturday I was late doing the shopping, and he left it till Monday, sir."

"Who unwrapped it?"

"I did, sir. I always do."

"Did you notice anything out of the ordinary?"

"No, sir; leastwise, now I think of it, I did, sir. It was a peculiar smell about them, but I put it down to some stuff they had been using in the wash, sir."

"Ah!" breathed Blake. "I don't imagine you are anything of an expert in perfumes, Mrs. Green, but try to remember what the smell was like. Have you ever smelt a poppy?"

"Oh, yes, sir! I have some Shirleys in the back garden."

Blake smiled slightly.

"I didn't mean those exactly. Wait, though! Did you ever smell opium?"

"Yes, sir, I have!" cried the woman excitedly. "And, now I come to think of it, sir, the smell on Tom's shirts was something like it."

Blake rose, and again placed his hand on her shoulder.

"That's all I intend asking you tonight, Mrs. Green. I will, as I said, take these drawings with me. Meanwhile, do nothing, say nothing. I know you will find it hard without him, but try to bear up. On my part, I will let you know just what conclusions I have reached as soon as possible."

"Oh, you are very good, sir, and may Heaven bless you!"

Escaping from her trembling thanks, Blake stuffed the drawings in his pocket and departed.

Instead of making his way at once in order to find a taxi, however, he sauntered slowly along the street until he had passed the Chinese laundry two blocks farther down. In one glance he got the name at one side of the door, the number, and a mental photograph of its appearance and those of the adjoining buildings. Then he kept on in the same casual way until he caught a stray taxi.

It was nearly five when he reached Baker Street, and on opening the consulting-room door he stood in amazement at the disordered scene which presented itself.

Several small chairs were overturned, a tabouret, on which had stood his smoking paraphernalia, was upended, and the general appearance gave every evidence of having been the scene of a struggle.

As he entered Pedro emerged from the dressing-room and greeted him affectionately, but of Tinker there was no sign.

Instinctively Blake glanced at the Japanese idol on the mantel, and, reading the signal of its face to the wall, he crossed the room and pressed a spring in the bottom.

The top half of the idol swung slowly around, and thrusting in his hand he drew out Tinker's note. Rapidly tearing open the flap of the envelope, he read, and as he did so an irritated frown creased his brow.

"Why didn't he remain here until I arrived?" he muttered. "The fact that the force I am working against has shown its hand in the visit of the man of whom Tinker speaks in his note, puts the seal to my conclusions. He was altogether too reckless in returning there to investigate, for as yet he has no idea of whom he is up against. However, he may be all right, and pick up some useful information."

Carefully tearing Tinker's letter to shreds, he touched a match to the pieces and tossed them in the grate.

Afterwards he walked to the desk, whereon lay the piece of the jacket which Pedro had torn from Wu Ling during the struggle. It was of the ordinary black material used in morning-coats, and, picking it up, Blake held it to Pedro's muzzle. An angry growl followed as the dog stiffened slightly and looked at his master.

"Good boy!" smiled Blake, pulling his ears. "You evidently recognise the scent, and have no love for the owner. That point may come in useful yet. But now to investigate the drawings. I have to see if there is anything resembling them in the books I got from Milne, Dodds & Co."

He drew out his knife, and cut the string of the parcel of books, and then, piling them on the floor beside the big chair, set to work.

Hour after hour went by, and still Blake pored over technical descriptions, making notes, underlining in a methodical manner, picking out every point which by any chance at all might have a bearing on the matter he was investigating.

When he had finished the last book and laid it down, he began to reexamine the points he had marked, in an endeavour to ferret out one which, by making the necessary allowances, might fit in a general way at least the vague description of the beetle as written by the late Sir George Halliday.

It was nearly midnight when the telephone rang, and at the other end he heard Professor Somers' voice.

"Hallo! Is that you, Mr. Blake?" he said.

"Yes," answered Blake. "I'm glad you called up. I was just about to try to get you."

"Ah! Have you discovered anything?"

"No," replied Blake; "nothing definite. I have, however, come across a remarkable coincidence in the shape of some drawings, and if possible will drop down and show them to you tomorrow. Have you discovered anything?"

"Not exactly, although I have hopes," replied the professor. "My records showed nothing, but this evening I got in touch with Dr Moore. He made the trip from Leh, overland, to Peking, you remember. Well, I gave him a general description of the beetle, and he says that on his last journey he heard several things which seemed to indicate the existence of such a beetle. He also said that by some of the tribes it was regarded with awe. He knew nothing, however, of its poisonous attributes, and seemed keen on learning if that were so."

"Well," remarked Blake, "I can tell you this much, professor. The beetle does exist. How far it coincides with the description Sir George gave I can't say yet, but of three facts I am almost certain. One is that it is yellow; the second that it has the needle-like horn in front; and the third that it is deadly poisonous, as Sir George said. Furthermore, I am of the opinion that it does not sting without provocation, and that in order to ensure its doing so it is lured on by a drug or perfume. That is, as yet, but a tentative theory which has to be proved, but I have discovered some very strong facts in support of it."

"Well, well," came back the professor's voice. "You are a remarkable man, Mr. Blake. How did you discover all that?"

"I cannot tell you over the 'phone, professor," laughed Blake, "but will do so when we meet. Good-night!"

With that Blake rang off, but even as he hung up the receiver he sat in tense silence, watching Pedro.

The big fellow had risen, and was standing, rigid and intent, before the dressing-room door. Something, Blake knew, had disturbed him, and, getting softly to his feet, Blake stepped stealthily across the floor.

Then he swiftly turned the handle of the dressing-room door, but no one was there. Hastening through into the bedroom, he switched on the lights and made an examination. There was nothing to be seen, however, and he turned to Pedro with puzzled brows.

"It is not like you to get suspicious over nothing, old chap," he muttered; "but I'm blest if there seems to have been anybody in here. The window is only open a couple of inches, and I surely would have heard it if anyone had opened or closed it."

Walking over to the window, Blake threw it up and leaned out. The street was silent and deserted, and from the distance came a measured tread which he knew was that of the policeman on the beat.

"You're developing nerves, old chap," he said, closing the window to within its two inches of the sill.

Had Blake dashed through while he was still talking with the professor, however, he would have seen that Pedro's instincts had not betrayed him, even though the dressing-room had been between him and the bedroom. For, during the telephone conversation, a stealthy, almond-eyed figure had softly raised the sash, crept through the window, and stolen across to the bed.

There the intruder had thrust his hand under the pillow-slip of one of the pillows, and hastily retreating, had barely drawn down the window again, and slipping down a silken ladder gained the security of a dark area-way as Blake threw up the window.

Ignorant of this, Blake returned to the consulting-room, and, gathering up his notes, laid them on the desk. Then he sat down and began puzzling over Tinker's non-appearance.

By all odds the lad should have returned during the evening. If his second investigation of the place adjoining Sir George's had revealed anything which he had thought worth following up, he should have wired.

"Still," thought Blake, "he may not have had the opportunity to do so. At any rate, I wish I knew just where he is. He has no idea of the depths of cunning against which we are fighting. That they are Celestials there is now no shadow of a doubt, but the question is, what is their identity, and above all, what is their motive?

"I confess it baffles me to connect the death of Sir George Halliday and Tom Green with one and the same motive, but I feel certain that is so. People, even Celestials, don't take such elaborate precautions to ensure the death of a poor stoker unless they have a powerful motive.

"Is it possible that Sir George in a scientific way, and Tom Green in a casual way, stumbled on something in China which brought upon them the deadly enmity of powerful interests? I must confess it seems so, and another link is the fact that both men had but just returned from China.

"Again, it is not a usual occupation for a stoker on shore leave to spend his time in covering sheets of paper with crude drawings, and all of one thing. The mentality which was forced to do that was, without the shadow of a doubt, driven on by some vague, intangible fear, but nevertheless real, as events have proved.

"Almost to the last degree the method of death was the same, and mathematically it is impossible that the perpetrators should not be the same in each case, and that the motive should be different.

"But why — why? Until I know that it is impossible to connect up the threads which, though gradually being untangled, are still too weak to bear the strain of a definite theory. However, tomorrow may bring forth something further, and I myself will make an examination of the house adjoining Sir George's, which seems to have such remarkable tenants.

"It seems evident that in some way they have gained the knowledge that Sir George's death has not taken place without suspicion being aroused, and that I have been looking into matters. That argues that my identity is known, and explains the reason of the Chinaman visiting my rooms today, but with what purpose it is hard to say.

"At any rate, Tinker and Pedro baulked that move, but it behoves us to tread warily. I wish the lad had returned, but morning may bring him."

With this conclusion Blake rose and prepared to retire. First he wrote a note to Tinker against his return, telling the lad if he had discovered anything to wake him at once. This he put in the idol and turned the face to the wall.

Then, pulling Pedro's ears, he made his way into the bedroom.

With only his two hours' rest of the night before, and an extremely wearying day and evening, Blake was distinctly tired. He had found very early in his career as a detective that if he were to keep himself fit for business he must cultivate the faculty of being able to sleep in any place and at any time. In addition to this, it was a creed with him never to take worries or business to rest with him, and consequently, as soon as he had retired, he composed himself for sleep.

In five minutes he was breathing evenly, in half an hour he was completely wrapped in slumber. A full hour passed, however, before any sound or movement impinged on the regularity of his breathing.

At the end of that time, however, it came in the form of a stealthy hand creeping slowly over the sill through the two inches of space under the sash. First the fingers appeared, then the wrist and part of a yellow arm, but with that it stopped.

Slowly and silently the fingers unclosed, and a tiny metal case came into view. Then the wrinkled fingers moved cautiously about the smooth side, there was a soft click, the bottom of the case flew open, and as the hand holding it hastily withdrew, something dropped to the floor with a soft, metallic thud.

A moment later two hands appeared on the sill, the sash was gently lowered, the stealthy figure stole away into the night, and Sexton Blake was left alone in the dark room with a something on the floor under the window gazing forth with two tiny, sinister, beady eyes.

For another long hour it sat there motionless, while the man in the bed slept on, but as he turned over on his side with a deep sigh, suddenly a pungent perfume began filling the room.

The pin-like head of the thing under the window began suddenly waving about, a long needle-like horn in front quivering in an endeavour to locate the position of the odour which, like a magnet, would draw it.

Then, with a rustling of scaly wings, it began creeping rapidly across the floor until it reached the bed. There the clothes hung over, and, gripping them with its fly-like legs, the sinister thing crawled up and up until it reached the top. There the pungent odour met it with all its force, and straight as an arrow the awful thing crept up the bed towards Sexton Blake's face.

It had reached the clothes over Blake's chest, when suddenly something of a startling nature occurred. The door leading to the dressing-room, which had been almost closed, flew open with a terrific bang, and through the darkness shot a terrifying streak with hair on end, eyes fixed and blazing, and great red jaws foaming.

Its terrific spring carried it with crushing force on to Blake's chest, and with a startled exclamation the detective leaped up to find himself in a whirlwind tangle of legs and bedclothes.

Ferocious and straight as had been Pedro's mad spring, it had not been in time to prevent the thing from stinging, but it had been in time to alter the object of its sting, for just as Blake leaped up the beetle struck again and again, its horn burying itself in the drug-soaked pillow.

Throwing himself free, Blake sprang from the bed and switched on the light. Then he turned to witness a remarkable sight. Pedro, with every hair on his body still on end, was pawing and tearing at the bedclothes and pillows in a frenzied attempt to locate the thing, the presence of which he could feel.

Suddenly as Blake looked, he saw something of a vivid yellow colour flop from the edge of the bed and fall to the floor, where it lay still. Like a flash Pedro was after it, but Blake dashed forward, and just as the bloodhound's jaws came together with a terrific snap, Blake pulled him away. Then, pulling him to the door of the dressing-room, he thrust him out and closed the door.

His first thought was that the yellow thing on the floor had been killed by Pedro's frenzied attack, but then, Blake did not know of the power of the drug over the beetle, which, after luring it on, sent it almost at once into a state of coma.

On more closely investigating it, however, Blake saw that it was not injured, and, hastening through the door leading to the laboratory, he picked up a specimen bottle and returned to the bedroom. Picking up the beetle with a pair of fine tweezers, he popped it into the bottle and replaced the cork.

Then, putting the bottle away for the time being, he opened the door and called to Pedro, who had recovered from his frenzy. Blake bent down and laid his hand on the dog's head.

"Faithful, brave old chap!" he said huskily. "If it hadn't been for your instinct and bravery I would not have been here now. You have rendered me many services, old fellow, but never before have you saved me from a tighter shave than that of tonight. In your canine way you understood the menace of that yellow beetle, but I don't think even your animal instinct told you just how deadly it was. But now, Pedro, we will investigate and find out how that perfume came on my pillow."

As he spoke, Blake straightened up and approached the bed. Rearranging the tumbled clothes, he lifted up the pillow and made an examination of the part which was still saturated where the liquid had been poured on it.

"If that had been there when I went to bed," he muttered, "I must have noticed it immediately. The smell is too distinct to pass. That means that it was put there while I was asleep, and — Ah, what's this?"

His hand had come into contact with something hard in the pillow itself, and thrusting his hand down, he drew off the slip. There, in almost the very spot where his head would lie was a small slit, and thrusting in his fingers, he drew forth a tiny bottle. The feathers surrounding it were saturated like the slip, but there was still some liquid left in the bottle, and as he held it up, Blake saw how the trick had been worked.

"Very clever!" he muttered. "They get in here before I come to bed and put the bottle in the pillow. Instead of using a cork they pack the neck with cotton wool, and make it just tight enough to ensure a period of two or three hours before the liquid soaks through and saturates the pillow.

"But how about the beetle — ah!"

This as he swung around and saw the window closed tight.

"So Pedro was right, after all," he muttered; "and there was somebody in here while I was speaking on the 'phone. It was then, I presume, that they secreted the bottle, and then — now I see it all.

"After I had retired they returned and threw the beetle into the room, and then closed the window. The liquid may even then have worked through, or, on the other hand, the beetle may have been here alone with me in the room for some time. In any event it was well thought out, and stood little chance of failure.

"If the door leading to the dressing-room had been tightly closed as well as the one leading into the consulting-room, I would never have known what happened to me. But I think the subtlety and persistence of my unknown enemies is sufficient to convince me of their nationality, and I have at last a perfect live specimen of the Yellow Beetle."

Smiling with grim satisfaction. Blake picked up the phial containing the liquid, and the specimen bottle in which he had placed the beetle. After locking them carefully in the safe he sent Pedro to sleep on a rug under the window, and once more retiring, was soon asleep.

Blake was not fated to sleep in peace that night, however, for barely had daylight come when he was awakened by a violent ringing at the street door-bell.

Pedro growled and got to his feet, and Blake, slipping out of bed, put on his slippers and dressing-gown, and made his way through to the front door. On opening it, he glanced with surprise at Godfrey Carslake, who stood there looking half-demented.

"What is the trouble?" asked Blake quickly.

"Gertrude — Miss Halliday— has disappeared!" gasped Carslake.

"Come in!" said Blake grimly, and dragging him in, closed the door.

CHAPTER V.   Wu Ling Tries a Bold Move — Tinker in the 'Room of Madness'

When Tinker landed heavily at the feet of Wu Ling and his companion, he was half stunned by the fall, which would have been serious but for the soft turf. As the two Chinamen, startled for once out of their native calm, glanced at the lad who had apparently tumbled from nowhere, Tinker got to his feet.

Without any attempt at bluffing he turned like lightning, and made a running leap for the wall, grasping as he did so one of the overhanging branches of the trees, which it will be remembered had formed his hiding-place.

Startled though he was, Wu Ling was as quick as the lad, and as Tinker's legs drew upwards Wu Ling made a flying leap and clutched him by the ankles. He then rapped out a guttural command, and his companion, leaping also, caught Tinker around the waist.

Then, cling as he would, the lad was forced to relax his hold, for it was impossible to sustain the weight which was dragging at him. Slowly and painfully his hands slipped along the rough branch until finally he released his hold entirely and tumbled back into the arms of his captors. While the man who had grabbed him by the waist threw him over with a deft twist, and held his arm in a grip which forbade the slightest movement, Wu Ling bent and gazed for some moments into the lad's face.

"Why have you come here?" he asked suddenly, in perfect English. "Didn't you get enough before?"

"I might ask why you came to Baker Street and set on me with a knife as soon as I got inside the door," replied Tinker, who knew Wu Ling had recognised him, and that bluff was out of the question.

"It is my place to ask, and yours to answer," rejoined Wu Ling haughtily.

Then, turning to his companion, he said: "Take him inside, I will speak with him there. If he refuses, we will use methods which will make him do our bidding."

With an obsequious "Yes, Excellency", and a vicious twist of Tinker's arm the lad's captor dragged him to his feet and hurried him along in the shelter of the wall, until he reached the house. Then, opening the door, he hustled him through into a well-furnished library, followed at a more dignified pace by Wu Ling.

"Now then, my young friend," remarked Wu Ling gutturally, "you will be good enough to answer my questions."

"I might as well tell you at the start," replied Tinker, "that I don't know anything, and even if I did, I wouldn't tell you."

"Oh!" remarked Wu Ling pleasantly, as he raised his brows. "Just give his arm a preliminary twist, San."

The Chinaman who held Tinker brought the lad's arm behind him, and jerked it up his back until it rested at the back of the neck. Tinker stiffened under the excruciating pain which it caused, but eyed Wu Ling in silent defiance.

"Let it go now," ordered his inquisitor, and Tinker heaved an involuntary gasp of relief as the hold was relaxed.

"Now, my lad," went on Wu Ling, his accent remarkably free from slurring, "you have had the very slightest taste of what you will get if you refuse to answer my questions. Firstly, what connection have you with Mr. Sexton Blake, and what were both of you doing at the residence of Sir George Halliday last evening?"

"You seem to know more than I do," jerked Tinker.

"San," said Wu Ling imperturbably, as he lit a cigarette, "give him just a shade more this time — slowly, San, it is so much more effective."

Tinker's breath left him in the sudden pain of the torturing twist, but he was game, and closed his lips in a thin straight line.

"Easy now, San," remarked Wu Ling, and once more the pressure was relaxed. "We will pass that for the moment," went on Wu Ling. "If you refuse utterly to tell me what I wish to know, my lad, I have a method which will make you very glad to talk, and of which you can not even imagine the torture. Come now, what do you say?"

"You can do what you will," muttered Tinker. "I've told you I know nothing."

Wu Ling waved his hand.

"Take him away, San, and see that he is kept secure. Tonight I shall give him a taste of the glass-room, and if he retains his sanity, he will be only too pleased to speak. Go! Return here, I have things to say."

"Yes, Excellency," replied San; and, unceremoniously dragging Tinker after him, he descended to the cellar and thrust the lad into a dark stone-walled cellar and slammed the door, locking it after him.

Then he returned to the library where Wu Ling sat, and stood submissively waiting for his chief to speak.

"There is much to be done," began Wu Ling slowly.

"Yes, Excellency."

"In some way," went on Wu Ling, "suspicion has been roused as to the death of Halliday. I have looked up everything about this man Sexton Blake, and find he has the reputation of being the cleverest investigator of crime in Europe — probably in the world."

"Yes, Excellency."

"He was not at Halliday's last night by accident, and if there was any doubt about it, the fact that this lad came here this morning settles it.

"I went as fast as I could in the limousine from Limehouse to where this man Blake lives, in order to search the place and find out what I could. There was, as I told you, in the garden a cursed dog there, however, which blocked every move I attempted to make, and when I tried to knife him he jumped clear like a cat.

"Then, as I explained, this brat of a lad arrived, and we had a struggle. I considered it wiser for the moment to get clear, and make the attempt later; but it shows the persistency with which they are on the scent when this lad follows back here and conceals himself in the tree."

"Yes, Excellency."

"Now, we can't run any risk of having our great purpose spoiled by this man Blake. And he must be stopped. I will think over how we shall do it. Tonight, after he has had a taste of the glass-room, the lad will talk, and then we shall give him the Beetle. You should not have failed to get the papers from Halliday's library; but since you accomplished the decree of his death successfully, I pass that over for the present. But we must have every note and record he made regarding what he discovered in China. And, if the deck-hand on the junk is to be believed, it was Halliday who must have been present during our last meeting on it, where Foo Loo paid the penalty."

"He swore by the Beetle, Excellency."

"Yes, I know. Besides, we have other proof which makes it seem probable. At any rate, he has been swept away before he had an opportunity to disclose anything. But he must have notes still in existence.

"For a day or two, until he is buried, the house will be too full to make any attempt to secure them. But after that these English always have what they call "the reading of the will", and then all papers are gone over. We must have them before that. And I have a plan."

"May your unworthy servant ask what it is, Excellency?"

"Yes, San, for you are to carry it out. The funeral is to take place the day after tomorrow."

"Yes, Excellency."

"Therefore, we must act quickly. Tonight will be best. This is what you will do: At midnight get someone to assist you. Lay the board from the dividing-wall to the top of the balcony on the Halliday house, as you did before. Halliday's bedroom overlooks it, and he is no doubt there. Lift the window, and make your way into his room.

"Miss Halliday will be up and dressed, for I shall send a telegram to her saying an old friend is calling, and can only come at midnight, and will she wait up to see him? She will do so, and you are almost sure to find her up and dressed.

"Study your plan of the house well, and don't make any mistakes. Get her quickly, and bring over the plank at once. Then we can all get away, and by morning they are welcome to search here all they wish."

"And then, Excellency?"

"Then," smiled Wu Ling softly, "Miss Halliday is no doubt a dutiful daughter, and will pay any price in order to be set free in time for her father's funeral. That price, San, is the handing over of all her father's notes and records before she is freed, and I think the plan will be successful in achieving its purpose. Now go! I would think."

San bowed, and left to make his plans for the carrying out of his master's orders, and Wu Ling, once alone, settled back and closed his eyes.

Celestial though he was, with no trace of white blood in him, he looked as he lay back there a man accustomed to command and to be obeyed. His brow was broad and intelligent, his features reposeful and inscrutable, his head carried with dignity. And, far apart as the poles though they were, he had an indefinable air of power about him which reminded one of Sexton Blake.

What was passing behind those lowered lids no man knew, nor ever would. He might some day feel the effects, but of the intricacies of that deep Oriental mind probably the man who would read its mazes more than any other was the man who was destined to be his greatest foe — Sexton Blake.

And likewise Wu Ling was to discover, when he came to grips

with the man who was called a mathematical machine, that another mind than his was a maze of intricate thoughts.

He had sat for some time in motionless silence, when a low, hurried knock came at the door, and a Chinaman in native attire entered. Bowing low, he approached Wu Ling, and stood, with bent head, waiting for permission to speak. Wu Ling slowly opened his eyes and gazed at the man before him, who was one of the thousands who obeyed his slightest command.

"What is it?" he asked, after a pause.

"Oh, Excellency, I have news which your unworthy servant would tell you."

"Speak!" commanded Wu Ling. "Speak! And be brief."

"Oh, Excellency, this day I have followed from his home the man whom I shadowed last night. He left with a woman, and the woman, Excellency, was the mother of the man on whom I carried out the decree of the Beetle. This man Blake, Excellency, went to the woman's home, and remained some time. Then he left, Excellency, and walked past Looey Sing's laundry, and entered a taxi."

"Did he look at the laundry as he passed?" asked Wu Ling, in even tones.

"I think not, Excellency."

"Do you know what this means?" asked Wu Ling.

"Yes, Excellency. It means danger."

"Then you know what must be done?"

"Yes, Excellency. He must go."

"Yes, Sexton Blake must go at once. I will tell you how." Thereupon Wu Ling ordered the man to bring him paper and pencil from the desk. A moment later he was sketching a rough plan of Blake's rooms; and then, speaking in low, earnest tones, he was instructing the man to carry out the Beetle decree against Blake — which, as we have seen, would have succeeded only too well but for Pedro's timely interference.

     *   *   *   *   *

Sharp on the stroke of midnight two shadowy figures stole out of the back entrance of Wu Ling's temporary residence, and, hastening down the garden to the garage, they entered. A moment later they emerged, carrying a long plank, which had it been daylight, might have been seen to be padded with leather on one end.

Carrying it along beside the dividing-wall, they laid it down, and

San — the man in the lead — pulled himself up and peered over the wall.

All was silent on the Halliday side. A few dim lights shone in the windows, but that was all.

Softly San signalled to the other to push up the plank, while he sat astride the wall and steadied it. Up it went until over half was above the wall. San held it while the other gained a place beside him. It needed all their strength then to hoist the plank the rest of the way; but they had done it before, and knew exactly what to do. Bracing it, they lowered it slowly until, with a soft thud, the padded end rested on the edge of the Halliday balcony, where Pedro had found the mysterious finish of the scent the night before.

Without hesitation, San stood up and noiselessly crossed. On reaching the top of the balcony he paused a moment, and then crept stealthily up until he was crouching under the window of Sir George's room.

Under his expert fingers the sash presented few difficulties, and after lifting it softly, he crept through. Pausing inside, he drew out a bottle, and, saturating a handkerchief, thrust the bottle back, and stole towards the door.

Now was the ticklish time, and he knew it. But Wu Ling had decreed, and it never crossed San's mind to disobey. If disaster overtook him, he must suffer it — that was all.

But as he settled a long, crooked-bladed knife in his belt, it was evident he did not intend to have disaster overtake him without putting up a straggle.

He knew Wu Ling had sent a telegram under an assumed name, and it was probable that Miss Halliday would remain up to see the man who said he was an old friend of her father. But she might remain downstairs, and if so, it meant a risky wait until she came up.

On the other hand, being ill from the shock of her father's death, Wu Ling calculated that Miss Halliday would rest on the couch in her room until the visitor arrived. And later events proved him to be correct.

The Celestial had left nothing to chance in his plans for vengeance on Sir George. In the quiet hours of the night he had, bit by bit, visited, and made a plan of the main part of the house, and by the study of this plan San knew exactly where Miss Halliday's room was.

Softly opening the door of Sir George's room, he stepped into the dark hall, and moved silently along the thick carpet until he reached the door of Miss Halliday's room. It was closed, and for a bare moment the Celestial's eyes clouded.

He made his decision suddenly, however, for without hesitation he raised his hand and knocked softly. A soft rustle, and then steps in the next room told him the occupant evidently thought it was a servant to tell her her father's old friend had arrived. A moment later the door opened, and against the dim light of the room could be seen the wan figure of a girl dressed in black.

"Has he arrived?" she began, unable to see for a moment who was at the door.

Before she could say more, however, San leaped forward and held her in a grip of iron while he pressed the drug-saturated handkerchief against her face. She struggled vainly for a few moments, and then relaxed, falling back with closed eyes. The drug had worked quickly on her worn-out system.

Picking her up in his arms, San closed the door and sped silently along until he reached the door of Sir George's room. He passed through quickly, closing the door carefully and then the window.

With perfect coolness he shouldered his burden, and walked across the narrow plank until he reached the wall, where he silently handed his captive to the other man who had descended to the ground. He in his turn laid her down, then pulled himself up beside San.

With a sudden heave, they drew the plank back and bore down on it in order that the length on the Halliday side might not touch the ground.

Again they heaved and slid it softly back. Then, leaping to the ground, they picked it up, carried it to the garage, locked the door, and hastened to the prostrate girl who still lay on the ground.

*　　*　　*　　*　　*

Tinker had been dozing, and had no idea what time it was when the door of his prison was unlocked and he was dragged forth. Without speaking, his captors tied his hands behind him and gagged him with a soft ball of silk.

Then he was led upstairs, through the garden, and into the garage where two motors were standing. As he passed the limousine, he thought he caught sight of the black-garbed figure of a woman, but wasn't sure.

He had no opportunity to look again, however, for his captors led him to the second car — a big touring car.

There they tossed him like a sack of meal on the floor of the tonneau, and he could see nothing but the ceiling and the interior of the car.

He knew a trip of some sort was being contemplated, for he had seen several Chinamen in the garage. He little dreamed, however, that Wu Ling and his men were making a general exodus, and that the house adjoining Sir George's would see them no more.

Soon he felt the car moving, the lights of the garage were extinguished, a pause while he listened to the creaking of a gate, another pause during which he heard the other car drive through, and the gate closed, then they moved again, travelling at a rapid pace.

Tinker judged it to be about half an hour later when the car he was in came to a stop. Three Chinamen had been sitting in the tonneau, but with one accord they descended, and the lad knew they had reached the end of their journey for that night, at least.

Had there been any doubt in his mind, it was swept away as he was dragged forth, and found himself standing in a rough-looking shed, which was evidently being used as a temporary garage. The limousine had arrived first, for it was standing silent in the corner, while its former occupants were nowhere to be seen.

Up a rickety flight of stairs Tinker was pushed, until at the top one of his captors pressed aside a panel through which they stepped.

The room in which he found himself was certainly an improvement on the rough place below, for although not as luxurious as the study where he had seen Wu Ling in the afternoon, it was comfortably furnished.

Squatting on a pile of vivid yellow cushions, and garbed in rich Chinese garments, was a man whom at first he did not recognise, but after a moment he saw it was Wu Ling. The men who led him bowed in silence, and Tinker grudgingly admitted that the man certainly exhaled a certain power.

He had little time to make conjectures, however, for Wu Ling looked up and said evenly: "Have you decided to answer my questions?"

Tinker shook his head. He felt a sinister menace in the expression of the eyes into which he gazed, and for the first time since he had fallen into their hands, he felt that he was in a grip which would not easily let go. He was determined not to give in, however, and defiantly gazed back at Wu Ling.

If he expected Wu Ling to command his men to torture him, as he had been tortured in the afternoon, he was mistaken, for the Celestial did no such thing. On the contrary, he smiled pleasantly, and waved his hand.

"Take him to the glass-room," he said, and without another word Tinker was dragged out

The house had evidently been well arranged for its purpose, for Tinker found they passed through two more secret panels before they stood in a small, dark passage. Then one of his captors pressed a hidden button, the end of the passage seemed to slide away, and he blinked his eyes at the dazzling brilliance of what he saw.

One moment it looked like a huge apartment, and the next it looked like a tiny box. It was mirrored all over, with the exception of the floor; but the mirrors had been so arranged that it would be a very clever man indeed who could tell the size of the room. Blazing from dozens of points were brilliant electric bulbs, and as Tinker was thrust in, he saw the floor was of steel.

A moment later the panel had been snapped close, and he swung around; but to save his life he could not tell through which one he had come. There seemed to be hundreds of them, and he grew faint and giddy with the reeling mass.

He lowered his eyes to the floor in order to overcome his dizziness, when a panel behind him opened, and a hand stretched out.

He was dragged back, while a piece of cotton-wool, saturated with some pungent stuff, was fastened at his neck.

Then a low voice spoke in perfect English.

"This is the glass-room — the room of madness. Look about, and you will see where the floor ends. From here it looks as though it covered the room. But not so. Go to the edge and look over. What you see there is deadly poisonous. One is instant death. Hundreds will make your brain reel with madness. The glass which separates you from them is very thin. You can save yourself by calling out when you will speak. The perfume you smell will draw them to your throat as the magnet draws the needle. That is all!"

The grip was released. The panel slammed, and the amazed Tinker was left alone.

"What on earth did the voice mean about the floor ending?" he muttered. "What were the things it said I would see by looking over the edge? And what did he mean when he said the perfume would draw them? Probably all bluff. Well, they aren't going to frighten me with their silly mirrors."

Trying to convince himself that he felt no misgivings, Tinker slowly advanced, step by step, until he saw, with a start that the voice was right. The floor curved over, and ended abruptly.

Dropping to his knees, he peered over, but gave a gasp of horror, and drew back, sickened from what he saw.

Below him, and seemingly protected by a very thin barrier of glass, he had seen hundreds and hundreds of repulsive-looking yellow beetles crawling about with ghastly needle-like points waving madly about.

He turned his face away, but gasped again as they became suddenly mirrored on every side of him. He never knew that a hand outside the room had pressed a lever which cunningly altered the angle of the mirrors so that walls and ceilings reflected the awful mass of crawling things on every side.

The glare of the reflected light was painful, and Tinker crawled back from the edge and lay down with closed eyes. The silent fascination of what he had seen, however, conquered his resolve not to open them, and time and again he lifted his lids to gaze in sickening horror at the vistas of crawling yellow beetles which seemed everywhere.

Then he moved suddenly, and gasped again. The floor on which he had sat was quite cool when he entered. He was positive of that. Now, however, it was quite warm, and growing hotter every minute.

He remembered with a twinge that his shoes had been removed in the garage, and then in a flash he recalled something Blake had told him.

White as chalk he rose, and stood up, and his eyes filled with despair as he saw what Blake's story had suddenly caused him to expect.

Slowly — very slowly — the steel floor began to move, passing over the edge where it was curved like an endless belt. Blake had told him of the torture, and now he knew the meaning of the glass room. The floor would grow steadily hotter and hotter until he was compelled to keep dancing in order not to burn his feet.

The floor would move slowly for an hour, perhaps hours, but gradually, at stated intervals, it would increase its speed, until where at first he must walk to keep from going over the edge, he finally would be compelled to run.

If his torturers proposed to let him go mad or go over the edge, to fall crashing through the frail glass barrier into that crawling deadly mass below, he knew there was no hope for him.

However, he would not go over until every ounce of strength was gone. He shuddered again at the reflected horrors about him, but at that moment the floor grew unbearably hot, and ever so slightly increased its speed, and Tinker, who had been making only an occasional step, was now compelled to walk briskly, and lift his feet quickly from the hot floor in his awful race against death.

CHAPTER VI.   Inspector Thomas Receives a Surprise Summons — Blake in the Camp of the Enemy — Escape of Wu Ling — Conclusion

To say that Carslake was upset when he rushed around to Blake with the news that Gertrude Halliday had disappeared, was, to say the least, putting it mildly. On the night Sir George had so suddenly died he had been, on account of his connection with the family, greatly agitated; but Gertrude's disappearance had struck still nearer him, and Blake was forced to give him a strong drink of spirits before he could gain any sense from the incoherent tale which Carslake poured out.

"Now then," said Blake, "pull yourself together, and tell me just what has happened. You say Miss Halliday has disappeared. When did you find out? How did you discover it? Tell me everything."

"Well," replied Carslake, licking his dry lips, "it's this way. I was at the house last evening in order to finish the funeral arrangements. I was also endeavouring to cheer her up. About ten o'clock, her aunt, who has been there all day, brought in a telegram addressed to Gertrude. When she opened it she found that it apparently came from an old friend of her father, and—"

"Wait!" interrupted Blake. "Do you remember the wording of it?"

"Yes, I think so."

"Then repeat it."

"It went this way, I think: 'Just heard sad news. Am passing through city at midnight. Beg of you remain up, as am very anxious to call on way through. Your poor father and I were very old friends.'"

"And the signature?" asked Blake.

"Simeon Jones."

"H'm! That tells nothing! Go on!"

"Naturally," continued Carslake, "Gertrude at once decided to remain up, and meet her father's old friend, and consequently, instead of leaving at ten-thirty, as I had intended, it was about half-past eleven when I got away."

"Yes, yes, go on, man!" jerked Blake impatiently. "If things are as I think, every moment is precious."

"The next thing that happened," said Carslake, "was about two o'clock, when the telephone in my apartments began ringing like mad. On answering it I discovered it was Miss Halliday's aunt. She asked me to come round at once. I dressed as quickly as possible and while doing so, sent the night porter out for a taxi. When I arrived at the house I found everything in a terrible state of commotion. As far as I could gather this is what occurred.

"Gertrude's aunt, being very tired, had gone to her room. The servants had also retired with the exception of the old butler, who remained up in order to be on hand when Sir George's old friend arrived.

"Gertrude herself was lying down in her room fully dressed, and when the visitor came the butler was to call her. Well, when midnight came, and the expected caller did not arrive, the butler thought nothing of it, for many causes may have kept him late.

"It pulled around to one o'clock, and when the bell rang the butler went to the door, thinking it was he. Instead it was a messenger boy, with a message which he handed in, and then departed. It was addressed to Gertrude, and the butler went up at once with it.

"He knocked at the door of the room, but there was no answer.

"Thinking she had fallen asleep on the couch, he knocked louder, but still no reply. A third summons failed to rouse her, so he went along to her aunt's room. She answered his knock at once, and on hearing why he had roused her she went at once to Gertrude's room.

"Like the butler's, her knock received no reply, and she at once opened the door. A dim nightlight was burning, but of Gertrude there was no sign. She at once turned on the lights, but the room was empty.

"Mrs. Foulsham, her aunt, was not anxious even then, but the first thing she did was to tear open the message. It was signed "Simeon Jones", and merely said: "Regret unable after all to come."

"Of course — of course!" muttered Blake quickly. "However, go on!"

"Well, Mrs. Foulsham sent the butler downstairs to look for Gertrude, thinking she might have left her room to be down in the library. She herself made a hasty search upstairs, but there was no sign of her.

"When the butler came back and said she wasn't downstairs either, her aunt began to get worried. The servants were at once roused, and the house searched from top to bottom. They could not find the slightest trace of her, however, and then 'phoned to me.

"When I got there I made a search of the grounds as well, but it is as though she had simply vanished into the air."

"Were any of her hats or jackets missing?" asked Blake sharply.

"No. that's the peculiar thing. Her aunt has gone through her entire wardrobe, but beyond the black frock she was wearing, nothing else has been touched."

"Where was the butler between half-past eleven and one o'clock, when the messenger boy came?"

"He was on a seat in the front hall every moment of the time. He says he did not doze for a single moment, and that he can swear no one entered by the door, or ascended the front stairs."

"And the windows?" asked Blake.

"He himself locked every window as he always does, and when he examined them they were just as he had left them."

"I think I will make an examination as well," replied Blake drily. "With all due respect to the old butler I think I could spring a catch and fasten it again, without his being able to detect that it had occurred. However, Carslake, you seem to have told as much as you can, and now I will dress at once.

"It will be necessary for me to make an examination personally, but I think I have an idea as to the direction in which Miss Halliday has apparently so mysteriously disappeared."

"My heavens! Tell me, then!" cried Carslake hoarsely.

"One moment," said Blake, holding up his hand. "I said I had an idea, but until I know my theory to be correct you must be patient.

"Keep cool, Carslake, for if I am not very much mistaken, you are in for one of the most strenuous days you have ever experienced."

"I'll try," answered the harassed Carslake; "but it's jolly hard, believe me."

"I know —I know," replied Blake dreamily, as he turned and entered his dressing room.

Had Carslake been able to overhear what Blake said as he dressed, he would have been still more puzzled. In effect it would have told him nothing, but the latest development in the case had made for Blake a concrete fact of what had previously been but a tentative theory.

"I wondered, when I was examining the grounds," he muttered, "if the trail ended at the edge of the balcony, for the reason that a plank had bridged the space between it and the wall. Then, however, that theory rested principally on the character of the tenants occupying the adjoining place. Tinker's discoveries, and now Miss Halliday's disappearance, convince me that must be so. But I must tread warily, for their latest move proves the calibre of the other side.

"What on earth is their identity, and what is the motive? By the way, that reminds me: why hasn't Tinker returned? I trust he hasn't fallen into their hands. It will go desperately hard with him if he has."

Little did Blake realise as he went along to Tinker's room to make sure he hadn't returned, that at that very moment the lad was beginning his ghastly race against death on the hot floor of the mirrored room — truly, as the voice had said, 'the room of madness'.

When he returned to the consulting-room fully dressed, Blake wore a savage frown, and to Carslake's questions, he answered not at all.

"Have you a revolver?" he asked curtly.

"No, why?"

Without replying, Blake went to his desk, and drew out two, tossing one to Carslake.

"Put that in your pocket, your coat pocket," he ordered. "You may need it, and if you do you will need it urgently. Now come on!"

A moment later, with Pedro on the leash, and the fragment of Wu Ling's coat in his pocket, Blake led the way out, and hailed a taxi.

Silence reigned during the drive to Sir George's house, for Carslake was diffident about breaking through the other's cold reserve, and Blake was untangling a mass of threads, endeavouring to find the exact motive connecting up two certainties and one probability.

The certainties were the practically simultaneous attack on himself and Miss Halliday's disappearance. The probability was Tinker's having fallen into the hands of the enemy, and as he thought matters over, he grimly decided that was also more of a certainty than a probability.

On their arrival Blake went at once to the library, where Mrs. Foulsham sat in agitated anxiety. Most of the servants were gathered in the hall, and from their ranks Blake beckoned to the old butler. "Come in," he said briefly. "I wish to ask you a few questions."

The man obeyed, and Blake, turning to him, said: "Do you remember the appearance of the lad who was with me last evening?"

"Oh, yes, sir!" cried the old man excitedly. "And I clean forgot about it until this minute. There has been so much happening, sir," he added apologetically.

"Forgot about what?" asked Blake curtly.

"Why, sir, he came here this afternoon and asked permission to go through to the garden, sir."

"Ah! and how long did he remain there?"

"I —I don't know, sir. I led him through the library and left him on the terrace. He never came back through the house, sir. He must have gone out by the lane in the rear."

"Very well, that will do," jerked Blake, who knew only too well now that the lad had not gone out by the lane.

As the old butler retired, Blake turned to Mrs. Foulsham, who was preparing to launch upon him an avalanche of questions.

"I can tell you nothing yet, Mrs. Foulsham," he said quietly. "I have several theories which require that no time should be lost. Try to bear up until we know something definite."

As she began weeping silently, Blake turned to Carslake. "Take me upstairs," he said. "I wish to examine Miss Halliday's room."

Carslake turned and led the way along the hall and up the broad staircase. Pausing at Gertrude's door, he turned the handle and stood aside. Blake walked at once to the window which looked out on the garden, and then turned.

"What room looks out over the end of the balcony where the dog lost the trail the other night?" he asked sharply, for he had expected Miss Halliday's room to be that one.

"Oh, Sir George's," replied Carslake. "Until this morning he was there, but he is now in the drawing-room."

"I wish to see it," said Blake, and, guided by Carslake, he went along the hall until they reached it.

Crossing to the window, Blake looked out, and his lips compressed in a thin, straight line as he saw it overlooked the spot on the roof of the balcony where Pedro had lost the scent.

The sill was a bare foot above it, and Blake was about to make an examination of the catch when Pedro, whose leash Carslake had been holding, dropped his muzzle and began pulling.

"I say, what does he mean?" asked Carslake.

Blake turned and watched the bloodhound.

"He has merely saved me some time," he replied grimly. "He recognises the scent on which he was before. It must be fairly strong. Let me see. It is now eight, and Miss Halliday disappeared between midnight and one o'clock. I think we shall find Pedro will lead us to the very spot at the end of the balcony where he stopped before."

Pedro had by now reached the window-sill, and throwing back the catch, Blake lifted the sash and stepped out. Then taking the leash from Carslake, he held it while Pedro leaped over the sill, and, with muzzle down, headed straight for the end of the balcony, finally stopping in almost the identical spot where the scent had ended before.

While he was worrying about endeavouring to follow it up, Blake, knowing his efforts would be useless, held the leash slackly, and stood gazing over the dividing wall before him.

From where he stood he could see almost the full stretch of the garden on the other side, and far down near the lane entrance a garage. Suddenly he pulled Pedro back and turned to Carslake.

"Here, hold the leash! I wish to make an examination of the window-catch."

The wondering Carslake took the leash, while Blake stepped back through the window and drew down the sash. Then, with his powerful pocket-glass, he made a minute examination of the catch, the hard, dry glitter appearing in his eyes as he saw two faint scratches on the brass which told him, as plainly as though he had been there when it happened, exactly how the window had been forced.

Then, lifting the sash again, he took the leash and motioned Carslake to follow him.

Down the stairs went Blake, and pausing only long enough to pick up their hats, he led the way out to the front door.

As he gained the street he saw in the distance Kelly, the policeman on the beat, and, with a muttered word to Carslake, hurried along.

"Good-morning, Mr. Blake!" exclaimed Kelly, as Blake came up. "You and Tinker seem to be spending a lot of time around here lately."

Blake smiled and went straight to the point.

"See here, Kelly!" he said. "I want you to come along with me. I'm going to make a call at that house next to Sir George Halliday's, and I want you with me."

"Why, that was the one Tinker was interested in," said Kelly, in surprise. "What! have the Chinese been up to anything?"

"You'll know later," replied Blake. "Come along, and let's lose no time."

With Kelly added to their number, Blake led the way up the steps of the big house and pressed the bell. For a few moments they waited, but as no answer came he pressed it again and again. Still only silence met them, and after several minutes of this Blake turned to the others.

"Wait here," he said. "I'll take Pedro and step through Sir George's house to the garden. From there I can get over the wall and try the back door. I'm afraid, however, the birds have flown."

Without waiting for their reply, Blake dashed down the steps and back through Sir George's house. Then, telling one of the servants to bring a ladder, he kept on until he reached the dividing wall. In a few moments the servant came running up with a small ladder, and hoisting Pedro up, Blake tumbled over after him.

Still running, he made for the back door, but found when he reached it that it was wide open. Inside all was silent, and without pausing to make an examination, he hurried along and unlocked the front door.

"I was right," he jerked, as Kelly and Carslake entered. "They are gone. Kelly, go into the library and see if there is a 'phone. If there is, ring up Inspector Thomas at Scotland Yard and tell him I wish to speak to him. You, Carslake, go upstairs and make a search there. I don't imagine you will find anything, but make sure. Have your revolver handy in case of emergencies. I will take the rooms on this floor."

As Kelly hastened to the library and Carslake leaped up the stairs, Blake took Pedro and started through the drawing-room. As he feared, however, both his search and Carslake's were abortive of result, and when they arrived at the library Kelly seemed the only one to have had any success, for he had found a 'phone, and Inspector Thomas was on the wire.

Blake picked up the receiver and bent down: "Hallo, inspector! This is Blake speaking."

"Yes?" came back the inspector's voice.

"Can you manage to come to Baker Street inside half an hour?" went on Blake.

"What is it?" asked the inspector.

"It's something big," jerked Blake. "I haven't any time for explanations now. Will you come?"

"Surely. I'll be there to the minute."

"All right," and Blake rang off.

"Now for the garden," he said, turning to Kelly. "Keep your eyes open for a plank of a good length. I'm anxious to know if there is one about. Carslake, you come with me. We will look through the garage."

"Oh, by the way!" broke in Kelly. "When I relieved at six this morning, the man on night-duty told me two motor-cars — one a limousine and the other a big touring-car — had come from the lane about one o'clock in the night."

"Why didn't you say so?" asked Blake irritably. "That gives us the exact hour when they cleared out, and means more than ever that we have no time to lose."

He turned as he spoke and led the way through the back door.

While Kelly began an examination of the garden, Blake and Carslake walked down and entered the garage. Almost the first thing Blake saw was a long, narrow plank, one end of which was padded with leather. After the briefest of examinations he turned and hastened out, with Carslake following and looking at Blake as though the detective had suddenly lost his senses.

Blake called to Kelly, who was across at the other side of the garden: "Lock the door of that garage," he ordered, "and put a seal on it. Then you had better keep your eye on the place, Kelly, until you hear from Inspector Thomas. Meanwhile, if any Chinamen of any description whatsoever approach the place, arrest them on sight. I'll guarantee sufficient cause."

"All right, Mr. Blake," replied the policeman. "I don't know what the game is, but I'll do as you say, pending instructions."

Blake nodded, and, signing to Carslake, hurried back through the empty house to the street.

"Do you wish to see this thing through?" he asked, turning to his companion.

"Rather!" replied the other savagely. "But—"

"Then ask no questions," rapped Blake. "We have no time for anything but action. Come; we will take this taxi."

Blake held up his hand to a passing cab, and, giving the Baker Street address, motioned Carslake to enter. On their arrival at Baker Street, Blake told the driver to wait, and, hurrying in, he waved Carslake into a chair.

"Wait here," he said. "If Inspector Thomas comes tell him I

won't be many minutes."

He hastened on through into the dressing-room, and there began rapidly to disrobe. From his exhaustive stock of disguises he chose that of a Chinaman, the disguise which several times before had proved so valuable in Limehouse, in half the Chinese quarters through the world, as well as in China itself.

Taken all in all, it was one of the most difficult of disguises to assume, for in order to pass muster it must be correct to the last detail. The eyes which would search him from head to foot were not eyes which saw only the surface, but which analysed and dissected. Consequently, it was only Blake's masterly capacity for detail, his perfect adaptability to the disguise, and his flawless command of the language which lent to his disguise the necessary value.

When he had completed his work he gazed at himself in the glass, and smiled a grim smile of satisfaction. Then he assumed once more the look which by pigments he had created, and, throwing open the door, stalked out.

Inspector Thomas had arrived while Blake was changing, and as the sleek-looking Celestial advanced into the consulting-room both he and Carslake leaped to their feet in consternation.

Blake smiled, and waved his hand: "Be seated, gentlemen. I see my efforts have proved successful."

"Well, by heavens, Blake, you are the limit!" gasped the inspector. "But why did you wish to see me?"

"Good, inspector," remarked Blake, seating himself at the desk. "I like to see your anxiety to come to the point. How soon can you get together a dozen men and motor them through to Limehouse?"

"I don't understand," replied the inspector.

Rapidly Blake sketched as much as he himself knew of the case he was on, omitting all details. Then as he finished he said: "So you see, inspector, although I haven't the faintest idea where the gang is, I am positive it is in Limehouse, and I think I can find them. Now, how soon can you get your men together?"

"Twenty minutes," answered the inspector promptly.

"Very well," went on Blake. "I wouldn't bring less than ten, for I am under the impression the gang is of no small proportions, and, from what I have seen of their methods, I think the lengths to which they are prepared to go are equally formidable. As I told you, inspector, I don't know who they are or what their motive is; but, in view of the facts I have succeeded in gathering, I think a prompt raid is essential. Now this is my plan.

"Carslake will take Pedro and go with you. Get your men together, and pile them into a motor. Then, if you proceed straight to Limehouse and turn down Limehill Lane which runs parallel to Belmere Road, you will come to the widow Green's house, which is the fifth from the further end.

"Go in the back way, and get her to place you where you can see me pass. I will saunter down Belmere Road until I reach the Chinese laundry two blocks down. Watch me when I go in, and if I come out with another Celestial, follow us. On your success in doing this the whole thing depends, for if you fail I have no doubt I shall never escape alive.

"As soon as you see me enter a house have your men surround it on all sides, and then do nothing until something happens inside. If you hear a revolver-shot you will know that is a signal to raid, and when you do, lose no time. Everything will depend on it. And don't forget, inspector, if, as I think, Sir George Halliday's murderer is there as well as his daughter, the capture will be a great feather in your cap."

"I certainly appreciate your letting me in on this, Mr. Blake," answered the inspector. "You can bank on my carrying out my end of it in every point," he added fervently.

"Very well," said Blake. "If you will go now, and take Carslake, I will get away after you. Oh, by the way, Carslake, if I do gain admittance to the house which I think exists, and if a raid should take place, keep Pedro on the leash until you find me and then free him. He will do as good work as a man if necessary."

Carslake promised he would do so, and, gratefully shaking hands, followed the inspector.

When they had gone Blake sat in deep thought for some time. Then he rose, and got the piece of coat which he had taken with him earlier in the morning. For some moments he contemplated it, then he stuck it in his jacket.

"I don't think it will be of any use now!" he muttered; "but it won't do to neglect a single thread."

Slowly he walked over and opened the safe. Lifting out the specimen bottle in which he had placed the Beetle the night before, he carried it to the window and held it up.

The Beetle had quite recovered from the state of coma into which the drug had cast it, and though he was accustomed to many strange things a thrill went up Blake's spine as for the first time the sinister creature and himself were face to face.

"I'm just as well pleased that you are safely in there," he muttered. "But, gad, what a creature you are!"

In the glint of morning sun the beetle's scaly wings shone like burnished gold. Its beady eyes glared malevolently through the glass at him, and the needle-like horn waved about angrily.

Blake gazed at it curiously for some moments; then, seeing that the cork was secure, he thrust the bottle in his jacket.

After that he slipped an extra clip of cartridges in beside his automatic, swung round, and made for the door.

Blake sat well back in the taxi until he reached the very fringe of Limehouse. There he directed the driver to continue on to the end of Belmere Road, when he descended.

A moment later there sauntered down through Belmere Road a well-dressed Celestial, with sleepy-looking almond eyes, and a yellow cigarette in his lips. The coolie class who passed him gazed at him respectfully, for his dress was of the superior caste, and his manner truly typical of that degree.

He kept on for several blocks, and had anyone been closely watching the front window of a certain small house, they might have seen a stealthy hand part the curtains, and a peak-capped, blue-uniformed man peer through. For a bare moment his eyes met the sleepy ones of the Celestial, then the Chinaman sauntered on, and the curtains fell into place again.

For two blocks more the Chinaman walked on until he reached a laundry, at one side of the door of which was the sign 'Looey Sing'. Here he turned, and, pushing open the door, which jangled a harsh bell as he did so, he shuffled in, and stood at the counter. Looey Sing himself happened to be industriously ironing collars, but as he looked up and saw the class of his visitor he hastily dropped the iron and advanced.

Contrary to the usual custom, the Celestial who had just entered did not speak, but after casting his sleepy eyes about he thrust his hand inside his jacket and drew out a small bottle. Keeping it covered by his hand, he pushed it forward until it was directly under Looey Sing's nose. Then he lifted his hand, and as Looey Sing saw the yellow, scaly beetle which it contained he bent over in an attitude of submission.

"What would you command your servant to do, Excellency?" he asked, in low, guttural tones, as the other thrust the bottle back in his jacket.

"You have already done well," answered the newcomer slowly; "but I have great and urgent news for the master. I have hurried on to London to the address he gave me. He had left, however, and I would go to him."

"He left last night, Excellency," answered Looey Sing; "and is even now near."

"Ah," remarked the other slowly, "I must see him at once! By the Beetle, I must see him! You will conduct me to him!"

"I obey, Excellency. Will you grant your servant a moment?"

Blake — for it was he — nodded. "Be quick! My mission is urgent."

And so by his masterly knowledge of the Celestial nature, plus his correct estimate of the power of the beetle, and his command of the language, did Blake enlist Looey Sing's innocent aid.

A moment later, with Blake beside him, Looey Sing shuffled out and turned to the left. Then he swung to the right, and headed towards the river. As he did so several blue-garbed men slipped into Belmere Road, and hastened cautiously after.

For less than five minutes Looey Sing shuffled on until he came to a rickety-looking building. There he turned down a narrow odorous alley beside it until he reached a low door.

Pressing a hidden button the door flew open, and he stood aside while his companion entered. Although the man Looey Sing called 'Excellency' gazed about him with the same sleepy eyes, the laundry-man never knew that his companion's pulse had gone the barest trifle quicker as on entering he had seen a limousine and a big touring-car. His manner betrayed no sign that the sight meant anything to him as he impassively waited for Looey Sing to close the door.

After he had snapped it to, the laundryman turned, and with a "This way, Excellency!" led the way up a rickety flight of stairs. At the top he paused, and rapped on a panel. A low voice came from inside, bidding them in Chinese to enter.

Looey Sing pressed the secret button which released the panel, and as Blake entered he closed it and retreated down the stairs, to fall at once into the arms of Inspector Thomas and his men, who had lost no time in surrounding the building.

As soon as Blake entered the room he saw, sitting on a pile of vivid yellow cushions, a grave, dignified-looking Chinaman, who, he felt instinctively, was the man he sought.

His pulses hammered as he realised the fact, and he asked himself, had he, by the result of his mathematical analysis and deduction, coupled with pure audacity, finally reached the very source of the mysterious and deadly power which, as far as he knew, was but beginning to make itself felt in England? Had he by chance placed his hand on something big, something gigantic, which later would prove to have a bigger menace than any man knew? And by the same token could he, after all, capture them and nip the whole thing in the bud?

These and a dozen other questions chased through Blake's mind in the brief second in which his eyes met those of the man on the cushions. Then, in pursuance of his plan, he bowed his head submissively as Looey Sing had done to him, and waited for the other to speak.

Wu Ling studied the bent head thoughtfully. In the Brotherhood of the Yellow Beetle there were thousands — yes, millions whom he had never seen. The man before him must be one of the number, but his evident high caste caused the subtle mind of the Celestial to wonder for a moment. But, as the other's head remained bent and he made no move, Wu Ling spoke.

"The sign!" he said briefly.

For answer Blake thrust his hand inside his jacket, and drew out the bottle which had had such an instantaneous effect upon Looey Sing. Still keeping his head bent submissively, he held it out, and as Wu Ling saw it he said: "It is enough. Be seated. I will speak with you later."

Blake moved over to the pile of cushions indicated by Wu Ling, and, squatting down, half closed his eyes, looking for all the world like a carved image of Buddha.

Then Wu Ling clapped his hands, and for the third time Blake's pulse quickened as another Celestial entered, holding by the arm a white girl garbed in black, and, with an angry constriction of the heart, Blake recognised Gertrude Halliday.

For a moment his fingers ached to grip his automatic, and then and there bring things to a head. But he wished to know more, and besides, a delay might tell him whether Tinker had also fallen into their hands, whereas a precipitate move might cause the instant death of all three of them.

He watched, therefore, with lowered lids, while Gertrude Halliday was led before Wu Ling, and the poor, terrified, sorrowing girl never dreamed that the sleek-looking Celestial on the cushions at one side was the only man in London at the moment who could combat the power of the web in which she had become entangled, and rescue her, if such a thing were possible.

As she was brought up before Wu Ling he gazed at her impassively.

"I trust you have rested well," he said, in his unaccented English.

Gertrude made no reply, but waited.

"You, of course, realise, my dear young lady," went on Wu Ling, "that you have been brought here for a purpose."

Gertrude bowed, and still waited.

"That purpose, like every other purpose, has a cause, my friend, and the cause has a price — a price which will purchase your freedom."

"What is the price?" asked Gertrude, her lips trembling and her voice very low.

"I have reason to think," replied Wu Ling, "that your late father returned from the East with certain notes and memoranda to which he had no right. If he did, they are bound to be with his other papers, and the price of your freedom is as follows.

"You are to write a note requesting that all his papers be handed to the man who shall bear it. They will be brought here, and I myself will go over them. I pledge you my word that beyond retaining the notes I wish, I will hand you back all the others. It is now ten-thirty. If you despatch a note at once they can be here by noon, and your release will immediately follow. What is your answer?"

"My answer is 'No! Decidedly no!'" replied Gertrude, in quivering tones.

"Ah," remarked Wu Ling, in his deadly pleasant voice, "then I take it you have no desire to attend your father's funeral?"

"Oh," gasped Gertrude, "you couldn't — you wouldn't dare to do such a thing!"

"My dear young lady, the sooner you learn that I can and do intend doing exactly that, the sooner we shall come to terms!"

"You mean you — would — keep me a prisoner here like that?" she gasped.

"Your sense of perception is marvellous!" murmured Wu Ling.

"I can't purchase my freedom at such a price!" wailed Gertrude, breaking down. "Oh, won't you listen and set me free?"

Wu Ling's expression never altered.

"That sort of thing will do you no good," he said. "Come, answer at once! If you don't consent, I will not only keep you here until after the funeral, but send you secretly to China. That and nothing but that will I do. Now, what is your answer?"

"Then —I — con—" began Gertrude, terrified at the threat; but she broke off as the sleek-looking Chinaman at the side got slowly to his feet and swung round.

Then as the other gazed at him his sleepy eyes opened wide, and his indolent manner dropped from him like lightning. His hand dropped, and when it reappeared it held unshakingly a businesslike looking automatic of heavy calibre.

"Her answer is — no!" he said suavely. "Miss Halliday, you will not worry any more. I am a friend, and there are a dozen more outside."

Turning to Wu Ling, he said, in the same suave tones: "Since you are so emphatic about what you can and will do, let me inform you that I am equally so. It is my intention to make a clean hole in the very centre of your forehead if you so much as move a finger. In addition to that" — he jerked over his shoulder at the man holding Gertrude, who happened to be San — "I will end your career very suddenly if you try to leave."

Wu Ling, to do him justice, never changed expression in the faintest degree. Instead, he smiled his pleasant smile and said smoothly: "You are a brave man, and I think I can guess your identity — Sexton Blake. Am I right?"

Blake bowed ironically as Wu Ling continued: "It is evident that things were badly bungled last night. I was under the impression that long ere this you had paid the penalty."

"Instead, I gained admittance to you by using the instrument which I succeeded in capturing," murmured Blake, secretly admiring the quality of his foe.

"Ah, yes; the beetle!" replied Wu Ling. "Really, I think you are the only man living who has achieved such a thing. It is a pity, therefore, that you are fated to be dropped into several hundreds of them."

"Indeed!" replied Blake. "I think you are mistaken. I forgot to mention at this moment the house is entirely surrounded, and that by a prearranged signal my men will in a very few moments be coming up."

"I am glad you told me," replied Wu Ling. Then, in a sharp tone, he said: "San!"

Blake, knowing from the tone that some move was intended, swung sharply: but the wily San was not to be caught. Grasping Gertrude firmly by the arms, he held her forcibly in front of him, and, using her thus as a shield began backing towards the silken yellow draperies through which he had come.

Blake's jaws snapped like a steel trap as he saw what was happening, and for the moment disregarding San's move, he turned back to Wu Ling.

The cunning Celestial, however, had not wasted any time in taking advantage of Blake's turning. Momentary as it was, it gave him the opportunity he desired, and, even as Blake turned, Wu Ling's lithe, yellow-clad body shot upward and forward, with the force of a catapult.

Blake braced his legs and took the shock on his hip, then, as San vanished through the draperies with the terrified Gertrude, he pulled the trigger of his automatic.

A moment later the revolver went flying to the floor, while he and Wu Ling whirled about the room in a mad tangle of straining limbs and heaving chests, Blake trying to bring things to a sudden finish by a throat-hold, while Wu Ling strained every nerve to get at his knife.

Then, in the very midst of the struggle, both combatants fell apart in one of those unintentional mutual movements, and Blake's eyes gleamed as he saw Wu Ling suddenly assume a correct boxing attitude.

The detective was, for the moment, surprised at such an attitude in a Celestial, for it is by no means the Oriental method of fighting. He did not know then, however, that with his insatiable desire to learn every detail of the lives of the Occidentals, whom he hated, Wu Ling had trained long and hard, and was no mean exponent of the 'noble art'.

Blake was not slow to assume a like position, and once more the two Oriental-clad figures went at it — their methods strangely at variance with their garb.

Blake dropped his head in a cautious crouch, and took Wu Ling's hail of blows on his forearm. Then suddenly his right came up and his left shot out in a clean hook to the jaw.

As Wu Ling shuddered from the shock, Blake swayed back easily, and slid a vicious jab off his arm. Then his right shot out, catching Wu Ling on the shoulder, while his left fell a trifle short.

Barely had he swung back, when Wu Ling rushed to a clinch, hailing a stream of blows over Blake's shoulder, in an endeavour to use the unsportsmanlike kidney punch.

Blake blocked with his fists against Wu Ling's chest, and, as he gradually worked free from the clinch, he insinuated his right fist up and up until it was in a perfect line with his opponent's chin.

Then, as he finally pushed free, he whipped it up like a steel piston-rod, catching Wu Ling fair on the point. The impetus of the blow lifted the Celestial clean off his feet, and as he feebly dropped his hand to his knife, Blake drove a straight left to the face, which sent him like a bundle of broken chips into the corner, where he lay still.

Panting, but grimly pleased, Blake bent quickly and picked up his revolver.

At that moment the draperies parted, and a horde of Celestials, led by San, dashed in, just as a furious pounding came from outside.

Inspector Thomas and his men had heard the shot, but were unable to locate the secret panel which gave entrance into the room.

Blake knew he must reach that spot at all costs, and, unless he acted quickly, the horde of crazy Chinamen would block his way. Levelling his revolver, he dashed forward, but San and his men were not to be baulked. The sight of the illustrious Wu Ling lying crumpled up against the wall filled them with a frenzy, and with a low, ominous mutter, they drew their knives, and rushed forward.

Blake saw that unless he acted rapidly he was done for. Once before he had stood in a tight corner under a hail of knives thrown by the unerring aim of the Celestial, but then he had a companion to hurl them back.

He had no more time to think, however, for a knife shot straight through the air and cut the silken jacket where it touched his shoulder.

Dashing forward, he began firing the automatic, while a terrific hubbub broke out from the inspector and his men on the other side of the panel.

Then pandemonium reigned. To the accompaniment of curses, howls, poundings, flying knives, and the vicious spitting of the automatic, Blake rushed the gang and gained the panel. Risking a crooked blade in the back, he turned, and kicked on the panel, just as the assault from outside succeeded, and the inspector and his men tumbled in head over heels.

As they did so, a startling change took place. San and his men, instead of putting up any resistance, fled through the draperies, and Blake leaped to his feet.

"Quick!" he gasped, pushing two men towards Wu Ling. "Tie him up and take him out. He is the chief one."

Then, leaping forward, he cried: "Come on, inspector, with your men."

Something at that moment shot over the heads of all and landed beside Blake. It was Pedro, who had broken free from Carslake's hold, and side by side master and dog led the way.

Tearing the draperies aside Blake rushed on through a narrow corridor. At the end was a flight of stairs, and crowded together were the Celestials, evidently prepared for a last stand before fleeing. At this point Pedro left Blake and dashed down a side corridor, and Blake, pointing to the massed Chinamen, shouted: "On! on! don't let one escape."

A momentary hush followed, before the rush took place, and in the lull Blake heard a far-away voice shouting: "Help, guv'nor — help! I can't hold out!"

Blake's eyes blazed as he recognised Tinker's voice, and shouting to the inspector to lead the charge, he dashed down the corridor where Pedro had disappeared, knowing instinctively that the bloodhound had scented his young master. His brows knit in puzzlement as he reached the end, and found Pedro tearing and growling apparently at the bare wall. Knowing sufficient of the Oriental nature, however, to know that it was undoubtedly a panel, he rapped on it sharply, and was rewarded by a hollow sound. Then, from the other side, came Tinker's voice in weak accents: "Guv'nor! Guv'nor! I can't hold out. Miss Halliday is here, too."

"Hang on, Tinker," shouted Blake. "I'll be through in a minute."

Feverishly Blake searched the wall for the secret button which would open the panel. Each moment seemed like an eternity, but he gasped with relief as a point in the wall yielded to his fingers, and what was apparently the end of the corridor flew open.

He caught his breath and leaped forward, however, as the blazing light of the mirrored room flashed out at him. For a moment the horror of the sight shook him with tempestuous anger, but, as Pedro leaped forward, Blake grasped his collar and pulled him back. Then he dashed through the panel.

The sight which had met his eyes had told Blake in a flash what had happened. A hot dry wave came from the steel floor, which was now moving swiftly.

Although she had only been thrust into the mirrored room when San had escaped by using her as a shield, Gertrude was nearly exhausted in her endeavour to keep on the floor and not be swept over the curved edge into the mass of deadly beetles below.

Tinker had for hours and hours been a victim of its exquisite torture. First having had to walk briskly in order to keep on it, as its speed gradually increased, and as the steel grew hotter, he had been compelled to break into a dog-trot, and from that into a brisk run.

It was for all the world like a heated treadmill, and Blake knew only too well the horror and the torture of it. Mirrored on every side were the horrible crawling beetles, while at his throat was the saturated piece of cotton wool, which would, did he go over the edge through the thin glass, bring upon him the whole horde of deadly creatures. Even now, as Blake reached the room, he was perilously near the edge, but his master lost not a moment.

Grasping Gertrude, he unceremoniously dragged her clear into the passage, and then dashed in to Tinker's assistance. It seemed, however, that he would be too late, for, with a choking gasp, Tinker reeled, and slid towards the edge, carried onwards by the swiftly-moving floor.

Blake gasped and reached out, and just as the lad went over, he grasped him by the arm. For a bare moment there was a maddening suspense. Then Blake heaved, and as Tinker's toes scraped the fragile glass which was the only barrier between him and death, Blake swung him clear.

Truly, it was the 'room of madness'. Once over the edge, Blake trod the swiftly-moving floor until he got to the panel. As he did so, the flying figure of a Chinaman tore down the passage, and leaped for the button which would close the panel. Had he been possessed of the speed and strength of a dozen men, however, it would have been impossible for Blake to prevent the threatened calamity. But Pedro, with teeth bared, sprang forward straight as an arrow, his jaws coming together like a steel trap in the throat of the Chinaman.

Blake gained the safety of the corridor in the momentary respite and dragged Pedro free. As he did so, however, the Chinaman with a crimson stain on his jacket staggered to the other side of the corridor apparently to lean against it for support.

Blake saw all too late what he was really doing. He leaped forward, but not soon enough to prevent the Chinaman pressing another button.

Something inside the mirrored room dropped. A sudden wave of pungent perfume swept along the corridor and through the whole house, and then, as a splintering crash of glass followed, there came an angry rattle of scaly wings as the thin glass barrier imprisoning the beetles was broken and the whole mass sailed upwards.

With a lightning-like spring Blake picked up Gertrude and shouted: "Rip that wool from your throat, Tinker, and follow me. Our lives depend on it. Quick!"

Placing Gertrude over his shoulder, he dashed forward, followed by Tinker dragging Pedro, who seemed to freeze stiff as the horrible rustle of scaly wings met his ears.

When they reached the end of the corridor the other Celestials and the inspector's men were nowhere to be seen. Only Carslake was wandering about vainly searching for Gertrude, and as he saw Blake he dashed forward.

"Quick! Come on!" panted Blake, and Carslake had perforce to follow.

Through the room where he had fought with Wu Ling dashed Blake, and thrust Gertrude through the open panel. Then he pushed the others through and banged the panel, just as the angry whirring beetles flapped madly against it.

"Come on! Take Miss Halliday, Carslake. The brutes will be through that panel unless the odour in the house is strong enough to drug them first into insensibility."

He led the way down the rickety stairs, and as he turned into the temporary garage he saw on the floor the two men who had taken charge of Wu Ling, while only the limousine remained. The touring car had disappeared.

Vaguely apprehensive, Blake dragged them out into the yard, and as he did so, heard the sound of firing near the front. Hastening around with Tinker and Pedro, he was just in time to see the inspector and his men firing a fusillade of bullets at several Chinamen in the windows above, who in turn were firing back and keeping up a deadly hail of flashing knives.

Then, as though by a prearranged signal, every head disappeared, and Blake shouted: "Around to the back, inspector!"

Drawing his revolver, and slipping in a fresh clip he had brought, he tore round, while Tinker stopped only long enough to snatch a couple of knives from the ground.

What had become of Wu Ling Blake had no idea, nor had he time to wonder, for as he reached the rear alley from one end, and the inspector and his men from the other, the whole horde of Celestials poured out through the door armed to the teeth.

Then began a fight in the narrow alley which will go down for ever in the annals of Limehouse. Up and down it raged, the Chinamen fighting with the desperation born of a forlorn hope, while the Scotland Yard men were filled with a savage determination to bring things to a head quickly.

Then, in the very midst of the struggle, while bullets were zipping and knives flying, there came a sudden interruption. A ragged Celestial stumbled out of the garage, waved his arms weakly, and collapsed just as a terrific explosion shook the ground beneath their feet and sent the roof and walls crashing inwards.

In the hail of flying debris the Celestials made a concerted rush to break the barrier, but the inspector's men roped them in, and ten minutes later wounded and unwounded alike were lying bound, just as the flames spurted upwards from the wrecked building.

Blake and Tinker, who had been holding their end of the alley from being rushed, and covering the rear of the Celestials, were mopping their brows as the inspector hurried up.

"Gad! we got 'em," he said breathlessly. "This is a great haul, Blake. I thought once they were going to get clear."

"How?" asked Blake.

"Well! when you left us up in the corridor the fiends disappeared through some panel in the wall before we could reach them. I thought it was a secret way out and made for the alley, but they were nowhere to be seen. On getting around to the other side, though, we saw a ladder hanging from the window, and one of them was just preparing to descend. They drew back, however, and we opened fire. Then you rushed up. But what happened to you?"

"I'll tell you later," replied Blake. "What became of the fellow your two men were to look after?"

"I don't know," answered the inspector. "They were lying over there wounded. Come over, and we'll ask them."

Blake did so, but could get nothing from either of the men but a rambling tale. It seems that they picked Wu Ling up and carried him down the stairs into the garage, intending to bind him there.

At the head of the stairs, however, he seemed to suddenly come to life. One of the men he kicked viciously, sending him headlong to the bottom. Then, drawing his knife, he turned on the other. Over and over they rolled to the bottom, but Wu Ling landed on top, and, leaving his knife in the other's shoulder, he had leaped into the touring-car.

While the fight was raging up above he had started the car and apparently got clean away. The inspector's joy over the capture received a shock when Blake muttered savagely on hearing the news and turned curtly.

His brow cleared, however, as Carslake came up with Gertrude, who had recovered, and as the fire brigade rolled up at that moment the little party moved clear while the inspector and his men hastened to get their prisoners into the patrol-waggon, which had also arrived.

Blake and Tinker looked after Gertrude while Carslake procured a cab, and, piling in the whole party, left the scene.

"I'll see you later," said Blake to the inspector as he departed, and sinking back, closed his eyes.

On their arrival at the Halliday home Gertrude's aunt met them with a look of fright on her face.

"Oh!" she cried, "I am so glad you have come. But why have you brought this Chinaman? What does he want?"

Blake smiled grimly as Carslake explained that it was a disguise.

"But what has happened?" he asked.

"Not half an hour ago," she said, "a big motor stopped out in front. The butler answered the door, and a Chinaman rushed in. He went at once to the library and forced open the safe with something.

We didn't dare go near for he threatened to shoot us. I sent the butler for a policeman, and when he came in he rushed straight through.

"The Chinaman, however, got away by the French window, and climbed over the wall. The policeman followed him, but the other was too quick. He ran through Colonel Porter's house, and coming out of the front door, jumped into the car and drove off at once. The policeman has gone to report it."

"And you have discovered that he took some of Sir George's papers, I presume?" remarked Blake grimly.

"Oh, yes, but how did you know?"

Blake made no reply, but he and Gertrude exchanged glances of understanding.

Then, turning, he said: "Come, Tinker, let us be going."

*   *   *   *   *

On Blake's evidence San got the limit of the law for kidnapping Gertrude, but so persistently did the doctors hammer any suggestion of foul play in the death of Sir George and Tom Green, that Blake kept silent. In the absence of Sir George's notes, he really had only his own facts to go on, but as he thought of the reality of the Yellow Beetle, he vowed the future should bring him again face to face with the elusive Wu Ling. The rest of the captured gang were deported, but all trace seemed to have been lost of Wu Ling.

The only consolation Blake felt was three months later when he and Tinker attended the quiet wedding of Carslake and Gertrude, for the pallor of her drawn features had given place to a healthier flush, and Carslake looked manfully determined to make her happy.

Thus ended Sexton Blake's first struggle with Wu Ling, once prince of the realm, and now head of the movement which had evolved from the chaotic condition of affairs during the fall of the Manchu dynasty, and of whose purpose Sexton Blake was at present only dimly aware.

THE END.

[38700 WORDS]

* * *

Read in next week's "U. J." how Sexton Blake and Tinker played their part—a most potent part—in the present-day events in the Far East. The news of Sexton Blake versus Wu Ling, the power behind the war in China, gives a guarantee of a good yarn at any time.

But now, when the banner of revolt is raised and the whole of the East has been set aflame by the emissaries of Moscow, you are going to get something extraordinarily good. Next Thursday's story is the first of a magnificent series of four, each complete, and each a part of Blake's most exciting Eastern exploit.

The "U. J." has never offered anything better.

THIS is the COVER— the time for you to place a standing order is—NOW!

[This is an advertisement that appeared in UJ1223 9 April 1927. This could be a far different series or could just be updated for modernity. Certainly the titles are all different but Wu Ling and the Yellow Beetles are there! /drf]

www.ingramcontent.com/pod-product-compliance
Lightning Source LLC
Chambersburg PA
CBHW031854170626
46807CB00004B/1718